The Sympathy of All Things

a novel

Fay Guilian

New Way Press, September 2013
Walnut Creek, California

The Sympathy of All Things
by Fay Guilian

Sympathy of All Things / Fay Guilian – New Way Press

ISBN-13: 978-0615875965
ISBN-10: 0615875963

Cover design by: Fay Guilian

For information regarding special discounts for bulk purchases
Contact: info@newwaypress.com

Printed in the United States of America

Dedicated to my beautiful family, perseverance, the spirit of adventure and living a life of fullness.

"The collective unconscious is common to us all; it is the foundation of what the ancients called 'the sympathy of all things.'" ~ Carl Jung

Chapter 1

In the years since my time overseas, I have often wondered how fate and synchronicity lined up to create the events that shaped my life. But in 1981 I was unaware of the significance of those words, and most of the time was simply looking for the universe to give me a "do over." Of course now I realize that by deciding to move halfway around the world, some inner general was commanding me straight into the battlefield, and my "do over" had already begun.

When the door of the airplane opened, a smarter woman would have had a feeling of foreboding. She would have predicted a storm on the horizon. In Ohio, I had known hot, humid, summer days. They were the times we cooled ourselves off by running through the sprinklers. But sure as the heat came, we could feel a mighty thunderstorm would follow. This heat was even more ominous. It was heavier and thick as cream. When I reached the open air, a leaden veil of warmth covered my face and even before I started down the blinding silver stairs, sweat beaded across my forehead. I watched the tarmac melt before me. Oily and black, the misty vapors rose from the cracks, seeping, as if volcanic fire was sizzling beneath the surface.

"What's that say?" asked my three year old daughter Dana, pointing to the sign above the entrance of the air terminal.

"Mabuhay. Welcome to the Philippines," answered Jessie. Only she said, "Maah boo hay," and later we found out it was really *Mah boo hi.*

In the heat and humidity of midday, with bags and kids, and in the company of a few hundred others like me, I searched the sea of faces for the one that belonged to my husband.

Seeing the number of people waiting, I realized it would have been smart for him to have picked a meeting point…or at least hold a purple balloon. All the men were dressed in green fatigues and at least fifty of them were six feet tall, slimly built. But instead of Mike, in a corner, standing alone, I spotted a tiny young woman with dark chocolate brown hair. Looking at her posed beneath the only tree, she seemed completely out of place. I thought we sort of looked like sisters. Same height, both in our late twenties. Except that she was a lot thinner and way more stylish. In her pink button-down blouse and pressed blue jeans she should have been modeling for *Glamour* instead of scorching in the midday heat. As I got closer to her I was finally able to read the sign she held:

Holden Family

So Mike wasn't coming to meet us after all.

"Hi, I'm Leah Holden," I said as I walked up to her.

"These are my girls Jessie and Dana," I continued, not quite sure what else to add.

"Rose Morales." She held out her hand for me to shake.

"Soo," she said dragging out the *o* far too long, "they sent me down here to get you, 'cause our husbands are both on maneuvers and that means, as usual, I have nothin' but time on my hands."

I couldn't help but smile at her, mostly because she sounded a bit like Rosanne Rosannadana from *Saturday Night Live*.

"Yous'll be standin' here soon. The Officers' Wives Club loves to give us these stupid duties."

I don't know why, but my first impression was that she probably wouldn't like me, and from the looks of her, I doubted that we would have anything in common anyway. She had that weird New York accent, and I had always heard how rude New Yorkers were.

Rose didn't bother with any of the customary preliminaries like, "How was your flight?" She just ordered the three of us to "Get in," pointing to the open back of a Jeepney. She seemed proud to tell me we were taking a "special," which meant instead of crowding into the open bus with twenty other people and fighting for breathing room, this one was just for us. On the outside, the Jeepney was lime green and burgundy, with the words, *LOVELY II,* written across the front. In small cursive letters someone had scrawled "sweet lover" on the bottom where a license plate should have been. I think our vehicle was called Emilie, because the name was engraved on each side graced by three little hearts.

"Hang on," said Rose. "We're taking the short cut."

If I had known anything about Clark Air Base at that point, I would have known her shortcut took us a mile out of the way, but on that first day I simply gawked at the BX and Commissary shopping center as we made our way out Sapangbato Gate.

Off base the road bumped and bellowed. I sat in awe of the different faces. A moving sea of black hair belonging to a group of schoolgirls and colorful clothes hanging in the tropical sun. I pictured Earth as one of those globes sitting on a stand in a library. I imagined tiny people statues, like you'd see in a children's book. I watched as my little piece was picked up, moved, and placed with a group of figures that looked and sounded strangely unfamiliar.

"MOM.," yelled Jessie.

"WHAT?"

I sounded annoyed even to myself, but at least she snapped me back to reality.

"Why is that boy peeing on the building? Don't they have bathrooms here?"

For the first time, Rose smiled broadly.

"Welcome to the Philippines," she said, patting Jessie on the back. "Yous never know what you'll see here."

The Jeepney bounced over potholes and dodged stray cats, while men carrying trays on their heads walked along the edge of the road. Women washed clothes beside the riverbank that lined the base perimeter. Signs posted every few feet on the fence read – KEEP OUT., to keep out the natives, naturally.

Rose pointed to a dilapidated little shack just off base. "That is the neighborhood Sari Sari store. Like a 7-Eleven, only cheaper. But don't buy anything that doesn't come in a wrapper."

She made one of those faces that caused me

to wonder if I should try to eat anything bought from there at all.

"Over there's the guard station," she said. "See that guy?" She pointed to a teenager who looked to be about five feet. "He has one bullet in his gun." She turned to Jessie with a stern look. "And be careful, don't get him mad 'cause he doesn't know a thing about rifles, and that one hasn't been fired since we fought Korea. You never know when it will go off."

At least that was Rose's version.

It probably was true that the tiny Filipino security guard hadn't fired a gun in his entire life, but the rest, well, from Rose it wasn't easy to tell if the story was fact, fiction, or just an overzealous imagination.

Soon we turned back onto the base through the MacArthur Gate. A few hundred yards later Rose said, "I live over here."

She gestured towards a palm lined cul de sac dotted with buildings that could only be made in the tropics. "In one of the barns."

The "barns" were my dream of what home would be like in the Philippines. Sort of upscale Nipa Huts with the entire front made like a screened-in porch. They looked like bamboo boxes balancing on stilts. I was praying for a barn.

"You're over there," she said, "on the street next to mine. I can't believe how lucky yous are. Yous get one of the new houses. When we got here they hadn't even started buildin' them yet, so now we're stuck in one of these ancient things."

I lifted my head higher to see above the driver and there it was—our spanking new, American ranch style house. Freshly painted sea green to match the tropical foliage. I would have done anything to trade with Rose and live in a barn. I've never pictured myself as the ranch house type of girl, and I frankly didn't want any remnants of American life following me. Since I did give in and move here I at least wanted to make a clean break. I had to admit though it was better than our second floor apartment in Columbus. Anyway, as tired as I was, I had no strength to complain.

None of us even bothered to take much notice of our new house that day. We just found the nearest place to set down the bags and then each of us claimed a room as our own. My main requirement was the bed.

With the kids planted in their rooms and Mike having been there before we arrived, there was only one spot left I could call my own, and that was the bedroom farthest from the rest, sitting off from the front entrance. I especially liked the fact that it had its own small bath attached. If given first choice I probably would have picked that space anyway. Being eleven, Jessie was just happy to have a long hallway between us. With the kids' rooms at the back of the house, and Mike's study/bedroom on the other side of the kitchen, he was just far enough away that I could almost forget he lived with me.

Funny, as I think about it now, we never actually talked about having separate bedrooms. But given the state of our marriage, I doubt that any talking needed to be done. There were simply four rooms and it made sense to fill each one with a person. If Mike wasn't complaining, I certainly wouldn't.

He showed up sometime later that evening. I remember it was dark out and jet lag had taken hold so hard I could only lift my head long enough to give him a peck and show him that I brought the aftershave he had been begging for all month. I slept that night and half the next day. I couldn't tell you if he spent the night with me. All I cared about was sleep. Long, blissful, dreamy, tropical island sleep.

Chapter 2

Morning came and I awakened to still, warm air. I had followed Alice's rabbit and come out on the other side. What was to the left? What to the right? I stared out my front window until the landscape felt like home. Guavas hung from long lanky branches, and finger bananas, still green, grew in my neighbor's yard. I had done it. I had arrived in a place where I had no past, no name, no direction. I felt clean. Something inside had shifted. My senses were alert, my mind sharp, all at once all things were possible.

Satisfied that I wasn't dreaming, I began to take notice of the house. My house. Well, technically, the US government's house, but mine until we left the Philippines. I shuddered at the thought that I wouldn't be able to change the color of the icy white walls. But, I was allowed to change the wheat colored living room furniture, so I made a mental note that I would be sofa shopping ASAP.

I found our laundry room beside the back door. It stood looking lonely in its own little shed. We had a square yard and it so small I wondered if Dana would even have enough room to play in such a tiny area, but the truth is three-year-olds play anywhere. Near the stairs, just outside our kitchen was the secret hideout for the house girl. I peeked in her door to see what life was like in a maid's quarters, and as I did my hand rested on the handle of a steel gray water pump. With hot and cold running water, a washing machine, and a filter system we had no need for it, but never mind, I would take the tiny yard, and the water pump, because I had a house in the Philippines. And for the next four years America was a whole world away.

When I stepped through the kitchen door and finally saw our house girl, she was more grandma than girl. Marisol was short and pudgy with her hair in a thin waist length braid. Even though I greeted her, she didn't bother to introduce herself. She looked a bit vexed that I was invading her space. I caught her in the middle of cooking some itty-bitty fish that smelled so bad I couldn't believe the stench came from their little bodies. Later I found out that the "pish" had been sitting on the windowsill for the past few days to get them ripe enough to eat.

To let in some fresh air, I cranked the windows made of milky white plastic slats, which she closed as soon as I turned my back. I was so happy to see those cranked-open windows I didn't even care. They were the one and only item in that ranch house that reminded me I was living on an island.

About a week later, Marisol started talking to me, and when she did, I wished for the silent treatment again. She said she remembered World War II. She was twelve when the atomic bomb went off at Hiroshima and Nagasaki. As she poured my coffee, she relayed the story of how her whole family started praying when they saw the orange sky because they were sure it was the end of the world. Then while she served the oatmeal, she added the part about how the Japanese soldiers had raped all of the girls in her neighborhood.

"My nanay, she make me and my tree sisters roll in the fig shipt, so we can stink. Smell so bad, no man want for us. We see soldier, but we hide in ditch. They no come near us already."

Although it was hard to comprehend her Tinglish, I understood it well enough to know what she meant. When she told me those same Japanese soldiers had used babies as targets like in skeet shooting, breakfast was over for me.

After hearing her tales of woe, I felt terrible about what I had to do, but after two weeks of treating me like she was the mother and I was still a wayward teen, I had had enough. She ignored my demands that the girls not eat meat, and she insisted on waking me up at the crack of dawn. And God forbid if I tried to take a nap, she'd burst into my room with her broom and start sweeping around the bed until dust flew in my face. Then she would apologize endlessly for disturbing me.

I didn't believe for one minute that she really meant it when she said, "So sorry, Madam." Truth was, I knew she thought I was a typical lazy American wife. I couldn't prove it, but I had the suspicion that she might have been taking pleasure in provoking me.

When the time came to do the deed, I passed the job on to Mike. I didn't have the heart to fire an old woman who had almost been raped by the Japanese, seen the atom bomb and had watched babies being shot. I just couldn't see myself adding to her grief. Mike, on the other hand, simply laughed at me in annoyance, saying that I would have to take a firmer stand with the hired help.

I stood in the hallway between the kitchen and the living room while he explained to her that we wouldn't be needing her services anymore. That was really all there was to it. No reason. Certainly not the way I would have handled it. I would have needed to present some type of evidence as to why she wasn't doing a good job. But not him, he said go, and she went.

With no other options, I called Rose.

"I had to fire my maid," I told her.

I didn't mention the fact that I wasn't the one who actually did the firing.

Again, she said 'Welcome to the Philippines' and then she laughed. "It won't be the last time. Yous know they come and go like pizza delivery guys, right?"

Somehow, I imagined myself to be the only dissatisfied housewife who promptly dispatched her maid.

"Chica, forget it, they're all horrible. I had six before I got Connie. What did she do, steal? They all steal."

I was about to tell her that wasn't the problem, but she just kept going on and on.

"Don't worry. I'll have someone for you by noon."

At 1030 military time, I hurriedly went about straightening the house so the new maid wouldn't think I was such a slob. I had barely finished the living room when the doorbell rang and outside stood Rose with a young girl not much bigger than Jessie.

Lucy arrived dressed in skintight jeans and

a Red Lips Bar t-shirt. Her spaghetti straight pageboy made her look no more than eighteen, and I doubted if she was that. I wondered if it was even legal to hire her.

To every question I asked, she just answered, "Yes Madam," including the one about her age.

Rose told me Lucy hailed from the Bicol province, wherever that was. Somewhere near the Mayan volcano was her explanation when I asked. And all the time I'd thought the Mayan volcano was in Mexico.

She promised me Lucy was a hard worker and honest, although according to Rose no maid was ever really honest, so she reminded me that I must lock my jewelry.

I chuckled to myself at the thought of locking my macramé necklaces and puka shell earrings. But instead of making an issue of it I just nodded that I would.

I was sure she couldn't cook, but I couldn't have cared less. After smelling the concoctions that Marisol put together, I figured we were all better off if she didn't. The main thing I wanted was for her to be good with the girls, and since she had a great smile and was little more than a child herself, I supposed, at least, she would keep them entertained.

Since everyone had a maid, when there was nothing to talk about at the Officer's Club, you could always tell a good story about how completely incompetent your house girl was. By counting fingers and toes I found out Lucy was nineteen. But, I soon learned that *all* of the girls said they were nineteen. Whether they looked ten or fifty they never seemed to age beyond nineteen. I figured in Lucy's case, nineteen was probably close to the truth because it didn't take long to find out she knew nothing about keeping a house or raising kids. Then again, I had to admit, I didn't know much more.

But to me, her age was one of the attractive things about her. No more mothers for me. I had moved halfway across the world to be rid of people telling me how to live my life and commenting on every decision I made. The last thing I wanted was another mother who I paid to treat me like a child.

After the call for help with maid service, I could tell Rose intended to be a fixture around my house. Somehow, she hadn't read my signals, because although in the beginning I had misgivings about a friendship, she just decided that we were going to be friends and that was that. Early each morning she arrived with a different agenda. First, it was shopping at the commissary. On the way over Rose explained how maids could do a lot for you on Clark Air Base to make life easier, but they weren't allowed to go to the commissary. The country was ripe with black-market trade in the 1980's, and all of the things at the Dao market came directly out of our fully stocked Air Force commissary or the Base Exchange. And no, not just cigarettes and alcohol like I thought, we also had a surprisingly high turnover of Spam, and Delicious apples. I could just imagine what would have happened if they had opened the doors to housemaids.

She also decided to take me shopping for furniture. To that I said, "The sooner the better." As we walked down the dusty Perimeter Road heading for the furniture shops, in the corner of my eye, I spotted the Red Lips bar. It took me a minute before I made the connection. But looking at the bikini clad girls who hung in the doorway yelling to the GIs, "Hey you cherry boy? I give you good time. Five dollar okay? Me ok for you?" I didn't get the feeling that my little Lucy had a former life as a 'bar girl.' I thought she would have better English if she had worked as a prostitute.

I pointed to the sign. "Lucy has one of their t-shirts. You don't think she used to work there, do you?"

Rose spit her coconut juice all over the street, aiming perfectly so she wouldn't get any on her blouse.

"Loca," she said, "if she had been working

there, she would never go to work for you as a house girl. Do yous know how much they make?"

From what I heard it sounded like 'five dollar,' and that didn't seem like a whole lot, but then I guess if you think in terms of numbers, yeah, our 35-USD-per-month salary probably was a half-week's pay for one of those ladies.

"Besides," said Rose, "the t-shirts don't mean a thing. Everybody wears bar shirts here. Shit, yous'll be wearing one before the month is out."

The streets off base were loud and colorful. The energy gave me chills. So vibrant and completely invigorating. The outside was in direct opposition to the finely manicured streets on Clark. On base we lived a combat camouflage world– beige with spots of green. But out in the city, the music blared a different song for every bar. The lights blinked off and on, even in the daylight, and jeepneys whizzed by with no regard for oncoming cars. We traipsed through dirty back alleys that probably had no name. Grungy men stood behind a few wooden stumps and broken stalls that looked like lemonade stands. Rose told me they were the 'money changers.'

"Don't ever think about taking your dollars to the bank on base." Nodding in their direction she added, "They'll give yous almost double what you'd get inside."

Something about the whole setup didn't sound quite kosher, but I had no job and only a small allowance from Mike that I was entitled to because of my 'dependent wife' status, so I thought I might be willing to take a chance even still.

"Is that legal?," I asked.

"Probably not enough that you'd want anyone to catch you. Ya know what I mean? I'll show yous who I use and then just go to her. She knows about everything out here."

We rounded another alley, going what seemed to be farther and farther away from the approved GI locations outside the perimeter of the base. Clark had mapped out all the off-limit places pretty clearly and even in that horrible orientation I had to endure, they warned us about getting involved in back-alley businesses. I admit I could be a bit clueless at times, but not so much that I didn't recognize we had crossed some unmarked border a few yards back and ventured into unsavory territory.

Just as I had decided to tell Rose I wanted to go back to the base, she stopped in front of a stand that looked similar to the ones closer to the main road. They were making barbeque, and even for a vegetarian, the smell of the smoke was appetizing and welcoming. I had no idea what kind of meat they were cooking on the sticks...and thank God, I didn't. That part of the Philippines is known for its delicacy of barbequed dog meat.

The lady behind the stand was round with a short masculine haircut. Buzzed cut around her ears, almost military style. She smiled a big toothy grin in Rose's direction. I noticed her teeth didn't seem to fit her mouth, which made them look like poorly made dentures.

"Sooo, Leah, this is Baby." Rose said to me with a look that told me the meeting was an important one. "Baby is my friend and has taken care of me for three years now. When I need anything, I come to Baby. Isn't that right?" She turned in the woman's direction and smiled.

"Yes, Madam, you are good friend for Baby also."

"Okay. Soo, Baby? If my friend Leah needs something you take care of her too?

"Oh yes, Madam, you tell me she Okay. She Okay."

"Alright then Baby, we don't need nothin' today. We're just shopping for some furniture. Leah's only moved here a few weeks ago."

"Madam? You try my cousin furniture store on National Road, he give you best price, okay? Tell him you Baby's friend."

I hadn't quite gotten the hang of what

exactly Baby did other than the money changing. But she did do one thing very well. She guided us to her cousin's furniture store. His business was run out of a warehouse with no real showroom for the items he sold. Once we said 'Baby,' Rose and I were welcomed with mango juice, and told to roam around and look at any of the furniture being made in the building.

"You pick any style, Madam, and I make for you."

All I had to do was point to a picture in one of his books, tell him the color and it would be delivered in one week. Well, not really. One week in Filipino time meant more like one month, but that was okay with me. I had four years.

I found a beautiful living room set that was full of curved wood and looked like a rattan replica of a Queen Anne style sofa with chairs to match. I settled on a deep maroon for the cushions. At first I thought I wanted a redder red, but at the last second decided it was too bright for the heat of the Philippine sun. When it was all said and done, my new living room cost me all of 200 US dollars. And to this day, some folks still say I got ripped off.

Chapter 3

"Read this.," Rose said shoving the paper into my hand before she walked through the front door. "I got it at the education office this morning."

"LAMC—Los Angeles Metro College? They're having classes on base?" I read aloud:

Introduction to Business English

Accounting and Finance

Western Civilization

Beginning French

Anatomy 101

Sociology 101

"Soo, what do yous think?" Rose was practically jumping up out of her skin.

"You mean, we can go to college? I thought that was only for the military members," I said.

"Loca, you're as military as that husband of yours is and don't yous forget it. Besides it's free. Come on, let's do it."

It wasn't an easy thing for me to decide to

go back to school. If I did, this time it would be the sixth, yes, I said, *sixth,* attempt to finish what I had started when children and marriage to Mike sort of got in the way. Every time I said I was going back to school I either didn't, or I went about three weeks and that was the end of it. Something would snap, and I would stop attending class. Then I wouldn't tell Mike or anyone in my family that I had stopped 'cause I was too completely ashamed to say it out loud. But this time felt like it might be different. I was on the other side of the world, and all the other times I had been in Ohio where history would have had to be rewritten for me to succeed. In the Philippines, I could take a class or two. Maybe even finish one.

The first day of school I sang and pranced all over the house. I even mimicked Lucy while she did her coconut shell floor scrub. She got a great kick out of me shuffling my feet across the floor in step with her. At first, I didn't think there was any point to the coconut scrub. I sometimes watched as she hollowed out a coconut, put some floor wax in the shell, turned on her favorite music, and bounced around the room. It looked like an impossible way to wax the tiles, but after I slid across the living room on my bottom at breakneck speed, I was sold. I even told her she could lighten up on the wax.

Rose called me twice in the morning. She

was already preparing for her grand entrance that evening. After deciding on a white tee and a pair of khakis, she phoned once more.

"Leah, what do you think about the gray top and my black jeans?"

"They're nice," I said.

"What's wrong? Is it the jeans? Or the top?"

"Nothing is wrong with either of them Rose" I answered.

Rose was never impressed with my fashion advice, so I didn't know why she bothered to ask me. It's not that I didn't care, but I guess I didn't act like I cared enough. Anyway, I had my own choices to make.

Anatomy 101 would begin in a few hours. It was my first college course in over three years, and since I had screwed up every other attempt at higher education, this was a momentous step. Being the only one in three generations without a college degree was not something I took pride in. My family looked at it as downright failure, and a betrayal of the family legacy. I was embarrassed, too. Even though I liked to call myself a "free spirit," I would have been a happier one if I had a BA after my name.

Since the day I signed up for the course, I dreamt about what I would do once I had that degree. I decided that obstetrical nursing was a good vocation. I even thought about taking that a step further. Midwifery. I got a big laugh when I mentioned it to Mike. He was in the living room hanging out with a few guys from the unit when I announced that I would become a nurse midwife.

I don't know what I was thinking or why I just burst into the room like that, but I certainly learned my lesson about what to say to whom.

They couldn't stop laughing and I couldn't help thinking that one too many beers fueled the laughter. But I realized how stupid they all were, because I wasn't talking about the kind of midwife from back in the old days. The type that yells for a kitchen knife and a pot of boiling water. I meant the up-to-date, tech-savvy midwife who was making about $80,000 back home. It was a good plan regardless of what Mike and the rest of his buddies thought.

I chose a magenta tank top and jacket to match, maybe because I loved the word, *magenta,* as much as I loved the color. I added my best pair of faded jeans, ones with a couple of holes strategically placed in the right knee and left lower thigh area. And I had splurged, taken my last few pesos to get a new a haircut. My natural curls were sort of shaggy all over my head, bouncing every way but down.

I liked that cut. About three months later when, *Flashdance* came out, Jennifer Beals had the same hair. Everyone forgot I'd had it first.

When Rose came to the door, she had

changed again and instead of the grey shirt, she now wore a green, tailored blouse.

"It shows my shape more," she winked. "Yous never know."

"Big night," I said, thinking about my possible future. "This could be the first step to my new career."

I had a feeling Rose was thinking about something else altogether.

Chapter 4

Anatomy 101

Without a thought, I headed for the first seat, first row as you walk in the door. I had rehearsed mentally where I would sit in class for the past two weeks. Even before I signed up, I had chosen that spot. In my mind, it was the seat of high achievers. I would always be in direct contact with the professor. I would never be distracted by the others in class. Some of them would be dependent wife types like me, some military. None as serious about this course though. Yep, I chose the perfect place. I would be first to class, and sometimes, the last to leave.

I placed my textbook carefully on that wire shelf that all school chairs have. I laid my black notebook at just the right angle on my desk. A few doodles with the Bic to make sure the ink was running smoothly, and I was more awake than I had ever been and very ready to start.

I looked around the high school science lab while I waited. All of the classes from the LAMC met at Wagner High. I liked the fact that we had class in a real school building, instead of an office building or an airplane hangar.

Studying the periodic chart at the front of the class above the chalkboard, I occupied myself with a game of, "How Many Elements Can You Remember from High School Chemistry?" while the rest of the students filed into the room.

Dr. Asher made his appearance at exactly 1800 hours. Bifocals and all.

If you had to dream up the perfect image of a science teacher other than Jerry Lewis in *The Absent Minded Professor*, you would have come up with Dr. Horace Asher. For some reason, he brought a copy of the *Philippine Flyer* with him to class. I watched as he spent the next five minutes trying to fold it into a reasonable facsimile of a rectangle. He looked so nervous, taking books out of his briefcase, then putting the same ones back in again. By the time class started, my fear of being intimidated by the instructor had completely vanished.

Shortly after Asher began introducing himself, a couple of stragglers showed up. One was an MP who kind of swayed as he walked. I had visions of the Cisco Kid after a hard night at the O.K. Corral. The other guy I saw mostly as a blur, out of the corner of my eye. He was like a blue haze, all turquoise and tourmaline. I avoided looking up at him in the beginning.

What I did see from my seat in the front right corner of the room was the image of him taking a seat directly parallel to mine in the first chair, front row, left corner of the room.

When I finally got the courage to lift my head, I found an excuse to lower it just as fast. His eyes were zeroed in on mine, and in a moment of suspended animation, a bolt of electricity moved through my core.

Every time I turned away from him a force of energy would pull me back in that direction like a magnet attached to my brow. He reminded me of a Filipino in his coloring and features, but I also thought he had the strong, handsome bone structure of a Latino. I mused over the possibility that he was the dependent son of some officer. But then again, he seemed too old for that, so I studied his hair to see if there were signs of the telltale military haircut. Could be an Airman, I thought, but the cut wasn't quite up to the Uniformed Code of Military Justice dress code. A bit too shaggy around the edges.

During class, I tried my best to stay focused on the task at hand. When I lost my way, I remembered my brilliant career. It was almost impossible, but I managed to keep looking in the direction of the board long enough to get the assignment for our next meeting and to understand how militant our professor was about getting to class on time.

When we were dismissed, I had a choice. Wait for Rose to show up and rescue me or try to be the first one out of the room so that I could find out which direction the guy in blue headed off for after school.

What was I thinking? I didn't quite know what was wrong with me.

I decided it made sense to put my head down and keep it there until I felt certain he had left the building. Even with my face pressed in a book, I spotted the eagle tattoo on his right arm as he passed my desk.

He had his shirt sleeve rolled up to hold a pack of smokes like all the guys did in the fifties. It wasn't popular anymore, but then he didn't act as if popularity was his goal. He even sort of had that Fonzie look, only much softer.

"Soo, Loca, How'd it go?"

I hated 'Loca.'

Rose peered around the corner of the door while I was still studying patterns of gray and beige tile in the floor.

"Hey, are yous gonna sit there all night?"

I grabbed my books, more than happy to get out of that room.

On the way home, I couldn't stop thinking—about class, but mostly, about the guy in the front seat, furthest to my left.

If Rose had known me better, she would have noticed that I was off somewhere in another dimension. The guy in my class had completely thrown me off kilter. As much as I tried to stay focused on Dr. Asher and Anatomy 101, neither had much of a chance to compete for my attention that night. I had almost forgotten I was married.

Hard as it might be to believe, Rose also had a strange encounter that evening. Hers was with a tall handsome senior master sergeant, and never the shy one, she apparently had wasted no time in becoming better acquainted. The entire ride home, all I heard about was how she had met the man of her dreams.

From the stories Rose had told me, I already knew she and Juan were almost as bad off as me and Mike. Juan had run the bars a few too many times in the last few months and on one of those occasions he brought home an unwelcome visitor. The type that required two shots of Penicillin in the rear end. One for Juan and another for Rose.

Of course, Rose didn't take too kindly to having to go down to the VD clinic and sit in the waiting room with the assortment of men who had picked up souvenirs from the bar girls on Perimeter Road. It was the height of humiliation for her and I wasn't surprised she made Juan pay dearly for that little lapse in judgment. Not only did she keep him at arm's length for months, she took a stiletto packed in her purse down to the Ponderosa Bar and confronted the girl in the bathroom.

"Geez Rose, you could have killed her," I said.

"Naw, yous know what I did? I backed her up against the wall and put the knife to her throat, then I told her to go get herself fixed before some crazy-ass wife *did* kill her."

This coming from a woman who called me Loca.

But all the way home it was, "Leah, I'm in love."

"He rides a Harley and, he asked me if I want to go riding with him. I have never, swear to God, Hail Mary," she said putting her hand up as if she were taking a Girl Scout oath, "been so in love."

"Are you going?" I asked her.

"Going where?" She wasn't following her own conversation.

"Riding? On the bike?" I reminded her.

"Hell yeah. Why wouldn't I?"

"Because you're married?"

I should have known better than to mention the "M" word.

"The way Juan plays around, what do YOUS think I should do? Wait to find out about the next one?" she asked, tossing her head and waving her free hand.

"Or no, even better, wait until HE falls in love with one of them, and dumps me?"

At least Mike didn't cheat on me.

Maybe she was right. Maybe it was stupid to wait until Juan found someone else and left her.

"But you love Juan, don't you?"

"Loca, are you kidding me? What love there was went out with Juan when he went out whoring."

"You ever think of just leaving him?" I asked.

"Shit, every day of my miserable life. But not yet. Uncle Sam takes pretty good care of us. Ya know?"

She was right. Juan was a captain with three more years than Mike. Housing, dependent allowance, clothing, travel, maids. For a "dependent wife" to leave a man like that was pretty stupid unless there was a super good reason and some kind of backup plan.

"Anyhow, I can't leave until I've done my time. I need that ten years, Loca, and I've only got a few more to go. Just doing time, that's all."

All of us knew about that great government carrot—stay married to a serviceman for ten years and after that, you are entitled to benefits even if you are divorced.

"You make it sound like a prison sentence."

"And what?" she said, "you're gonna tell me it's not?"

But I had my own marriage dragons to slay. There were so many reasons I should have been content with Mike. He wasn't horribly unattractive or stupid, well sometimes he was rather stupid...but he did have the captain bars, and despite the lack of passion in my marriage, he wasn't usually unkind. He just wasn't affectionate. Or interested in me.

I knew if I never complained, and we lived in separate bedrooms for the next fifty years it would have been fine by him. He would have said he had a happy marriage. I had always thought men were more interested in sex than women, but just my luck, I married a monk.

If anyone was ripe for the picking, it was me. So many silly childhood fantasies colored the dull reality of my life inside that ranch house. I knew I was a daydreamer, and now most of fantasies were filled with thoughts of the guy from Anatomy 101.

I had never been so drawn to another human being before in my life, and the idea of it happening now seemed so plainly wrong. If I had been younger, unmarried, or even divorced, I would have been shouting to the rooftops about the man who had my mind racing. Who caused such an unexplainable reaction in me when I didn't even know his name. But despite my secret joy of simply knowing what it felt like to experience that kind of raw attraction for the first time, I had made this journey for other reasons. My commitment was to do my four years with Mike, and to get my life and maybe even my marriage in order. No matter how compelling, a flirtation with the handsome mysterious man in my first college course did not fit into that picture.

I couldn't give any hints away that I might be interested in someone other than my husband. I was having a hard enough time admitting it to myself. But the next class period, I made a conscious effort to listen when Asher called attendance. As I recall, that was the first and last university class I enrolled in where they ever even bothered to call roll. Michael Harrison. I still remember the twinge I felt when the professor called his name.

Next class, I gathered information. He rode a bicycle to school, as opposed to a "bike" like Rose's Lance. From the book he carried under his arm as he passed by me to get to his same seat, I learned he read Carl Jung, (whom I had never heard of, but all of a sudden had a burning desire to investigate) and, he was left-handed.

I knew, as sure as I knew something weird

was stirring in me, his being left-handed had to be a sign. For a man to truly understand me he must be like me, so being left-handed would be part of that. Maybe to some people it sounds crazy, but it was my version of the perfect mate. Some people want non-drinkers, some want men who dance. I wanted a lefty.

Rose didn't waste a minute getting Lance to take her on that motorcycle ride.

"I'm in love," I heard it from her daily. But Rose was well…Rose. So I couldn't get too worked up over her pronouncements.

"We went all over, back of the base, I was holding on to him, feeling those muscles, Loca, I am telling you the truth. He's the one."

"Maybe it's just infatuation. Rose," I said.

But even as I spoke, I was thinking about the object of my attraction. Was that infatuation, too?

"I don't know, maybe you shouldn't get too involved with this Lance guy," I cautioned. "I mean you don't know anything about him."

"I know he's not married."

"What you would do if he feels the same way about you?" I asked.

"What do you think I would do?"

She gave a look that said it all. Rose never seemed to hesitate. She always knew what she wanted. She didn't stop to tarry or debate in her head. She jumped right in. Damn the consequences.

"I thought you had it all planned out. You know, wait three years to get the allowance?"

"Uh huh, but if I marry Lance I don't have to wait. What would yous do?"

"I don't know, Rose," I said. "Even if I wanted to, I don't think I could...I guess if…."

I caught myself dreaming out loud.

"Loca. Yous aren't thinking about somebody else, are you?"

"Just wondering," I answered.

"Why?" She asked. "What the hell has he done?"

That was the problem. He had done nothing to make me even consider what I was considering daily. He was being the best Mike he knew how to be.

"OK, you know yous can't fool me, Sooo. Spill it."

Rose would have been a great lawyer. But, I evaded the questioning with a little manipulation of my own. God forbid, if the thoughts that had been rolling around in my head, start blurting out of my mouth. Better to change the subject back to Lance.

And at this point, she didn't care about anything else.

For the time being, I was safe.

I still hadn't told her about Michael Harrison.

Chapter 5

I remember being about ten years old, telling my mom that I would grow up and fall in love with a man named Michael. Mom's answer to that was;

"Sure, honey."

Her less than enthusiastic reply didn't faze me though, because I just knew his name would be Michael. Thinking about it now, that is probably part of the reason I married my husband. He had to be the right one. His name was Michael.

But all of a sudden, a new Michael enters and I recalled that talk with my mother. Was I supposed to fall in love with a different Michael? By now, I was certain it wasn't the one I had married. I was glad I hadn't caved into Rose's inquisition. Michael Harrison, for the moment, was my own private retreat from the more mundane world of being a "dependent wife" and I wanted to keep it that way.

No harm, no foul. Nothing had happened and probably nothing would. One thing I knew: I wasn't ready to talk about him. If I was reading the signs right, he seemed interested in me, too. All I really knew was that every time I raised my head out of the cocoon I had created, his eyes were glued in my direction. But then again, he would do this strange disappearing act as soon as we were dismissed. Cinderfella turned into a pumpkin at half-past nine.

What if I was imagining it? What if he was staring because I reminded him of his sister, or mother? It *was* possible. Or could it be some other ordinary reason like that? I might have totally misread the signs. Mike, the husband, said I did that sometimes.

The more I thought about him, the stronger the desire. It was bouncing back and forth from one side of the classroom to the other at the speed of light. At least coming from my direction it was surely palpable and I was becoming unnerved. The image of him flew across my brain too many times in a day for me to count. I started dancing to Olivia Newton John's "Let Get Physical." Lucy sensed strange things were stirring. Mike, the husband, of course, did not.

By the third week of class, both Rose and I had reasons other than Business English and

Anatomy 101 to motivate our love of learning. Rose seemed to be moving right along with her plan to snag Lance, and I of course, was trailing quite far behind with Michael Harrison. It wasn't easy for me to toy with the idea of 'cheating' on my husband. It wasn't something I did. Marriage for better or worse, and even though in my case it felt worse, I had made a commitment, and that meant being loyal.

I had complained even before Dana was born that we had no soul connection. A vow based on a big mistake. The first couple of months at Clark had been spent with my eyes on a whole new world, but it had done nothing to change the way I felt about life with my husband. We were definitely mismatched. I didn't dare say out loud what I had started to believe. The attraction that I felt for the new guy was way too strong; I think I realized even from the first day, that if given an opening, I would throw all caution out the door for a chance to be with him.

Chapter 6

When I finally did confess to Rose about what had been going on since the first day of class, she let out a big "I KNEW IT." The way she saw it, we were now conspirators in deception.

"I knew somethin' was going on. Loca yous, can't fool me. Look at the way you've been doin' your hair up and gettin' all cute each time we have class." She shook her finger in my face. "Soo, now what are YOUS gonna do?"

Unlike Rose, I had no plans. I was in the midst of a storm and was being carried away in it. I was actually afraid of where I would land.

"Well I'll tell yous what you're gonna do," she said. "First you've gotta get this guy to talk to you. Yous soo need my help."

Even though a voice inside told me it was the wrong thing to do, the voice was fading as the force of nature brewing outside grew and refused to be ignored. I felt helpless to fight it. As time went on, it felt silly to try.

Rose decided to launch the offense the very night she found out. As the designated driver to Wagner High each Monday and Wednesday, she was in control of where we went, and on this particular night I was a bit irritated because it was already 1740 hours when she picked me up, and she had decided to make a detour before class.

"Courage woman. That's what you need," she said as she sped around the corner. "We're making a pit stop to the Chicken Coop before class."

Everyone at Clark made pit stops to the Chicken Coop. Only not at 1740 when class started at 1800. The Chicken Coop had the look of a 1950s diner, complete with carhops. Like the rest of the population, I loved the food at the Chicken Coop, but we were late. I knew Asher would go ballistic and I also had an inkling Rose was working a plan. I wasn't sure what she had up her sleeve, but it surely spelled trouble and she looked determined. I didn't dare ask.

Before I could say anything, she had ordered.

"Two lemonades and a bag of onion rings."

Okay, not so bad, I thought. I can relate to that. If courage tasted like onion rings and lemonade I could go along with the program.

Just when I took comfort in the idea of the

onion rings, out came her silver flask. In my entire life I have never seen another person who owned one of those things other than Rose. She pointed to my cup of lemonade. "Drink some," she ordered.

Before I could take three gulps, Rose had grabbed my 16-ounce cup and poured a good portion of it out on the hot cement.

"Sorry," she apologized. "You were taking too long."

She refilled half the cup with Smirnoff's.

"You seriously want me to drink that?" I was afraid I would pass out in the middle of anatomy.

"Behold your courage." She announced holding the cup up for emphasis.

Before the straw touched my lips she screamed, "Don't drink it NOW, Loca. Wait. Sip a little. Your professor lets you guys have drinks, right?" She wasn't looking for a response.

"Slowly. Drink a little bit here and there. Yous don't want that man to be pickin' you up off the floor."

Now, that was a sobering thought, no matter how much Vodka she had put in the drink.

"When break comes you should be just about mellow enough to make the first move."

Good old Rose. Plotting like an expert.

"Then, take a couple of these onion rings and eat them so that you won't smell like booze."

"No I'll just smell like onions *and* booze." I was having visions of slurred words and stumbling over my feet.

Just as I arrived, Michael Harrison walked into the room in green. The boy in blue was wearing military fatigues. Stripes and all. Four of them to be exact. The mark of a Staff Sergeant.

We were doing the respiratory system.

I prayed Asher wouldn't decide to have us check pulses on each other. Mine was racing like a freight train going downhill without brakes. After what seemed like many hours of the perfunctory lecture, it happened.

"Okay class, let's take twenty." Asher uttered the dreaded words. The moment of truth had arrived. Could the sickness in the pit of my stomach have been from Rose's cocktail or was it pure panic?

He bolted out the door as usual. Why was he was so damned anti-social? I dropped my books and fell in behind, hoping to spy on him and find out exactly where he hid during break. I had forgotten my drink. I darted back up the hall, and in one swoop leaned around the corner, grabbed it and ran. Too late. That stupid, idiotic drink. He was out of sight. The

T-shaped corridor of the high school was remarkably white and wide. Too wide for a high school I thought, and definitely too bright. At the end of the hall I had to make a decision. Did he go to the left, which would have been the bathrooms, and the grassy hill behind the school, or to the right? That would be the parking lot, student canteen, and library. I made my decision based on thirst. The 'lemonade' had made my tongue hairy and thick, and I desperately needed water. Water fountain to the right.

"Are you going to be finished soon?"

The voice behind me sent a shiver down my legs. Without turning I knew who it belonged to. Funny how I knew. He had never uttered a word in class. Even when Asher called the role, he only raised his hand and forced the old man to look up over his glasses.

And now I had been caught watering like a moose.

"Yes," I wiped my lips with my shirtsleeve. "I'm finished."

Great impression.

He didn't want the fountain. "Hi, I'm Harris. I'm in your class."

"Oh," I said. "I thought your name was Michael." It came out before I had a chance to self-censor. Wonderful.

"It is," he said, smiling. "But my friends

have been calling me 'Harris' since I was a kid, and I guess it stuck."

"I'm Leah," I said coolly, trying to recover from the *faux pas*.

"I know," he laughed. "How do you like the class?"

Oh okay, so we were going to be caught in some inane banter about the class, the weather, the Philippines, and so on and so forth.

"Class is fine," I said impatiently. "How long have you been in the PI?"

"About a year and a half and you?" he replied.

"Almost three months. How long are you staying?"

"Another year and a half."

And then, from that place I have, that allows the mouth to open before thought intervenes, came the word, "Good."

Rose cackled all the way home. She thought my blunders were hysterical.

"I don't know how yous do it Loca. I give you one drink and you blubber all over yourself."

I was feeling embarrassed enough without her commentary. But as I sat in the tub that evening thinking about our first encounter, I remembered, when he heard me say, 'good,' he smiled. Maybe it wasn't so bad after all, because he gave me a genuine smile. Not one of those polite, 'that's nice' smiles, but a big, happy, 'I like what you said', kind of grin.

Or was it a, 'I like what you said 'cause you are funny and a bit childish,' kind of grin?

Ouch.

Chapter 7

Time between classes moved to a new beat after that. First slowing and sometimes stopping altogether. There were several hours of just watching the clock, looking in the mirror, trying on everything in the closet, and infinite moments daydreaming about what our next conversation would be like. The obsession with Harris kept growing. Even though he said he had always been Harris, I couldn't forget that he was really another Michael. I began to think having class only twice a week was some kind of cruel joke or comeuppance designed to frustrate and punish me for my immoral thoughts.

Rose was busy finding out all the small details about Lance. She talked about him incessantly. Lance was with the 31st Airborne, Lance worked on the flight simulators, Lance lived in Barrett Hall, and Lance rode his bike off base in the evenings.

On the other hand, I had no clue where Harris lived, worked, ate, or played.

I spent a lot of time peering out the passenger window, with Rose at the wheel, trying to spot a sort of Filipino looking, Staff Sergeant in fatigues, on an air base in the PI.

As you might imagine, that proved to be a pointless exercise.

"Didn't you ask him where he works?" Rose asked with her usual curtness. "Why didn't you look on his uniform? They always list the organization on their fatigues."

All I could say was, "No. I don't know, and yeah, I know." Truth be told, my nerves had been too shaky to ask those questions or even to focus on the uniform patches. Besides, thanks to Rose, I had also been too looped to think. Period.

"Let's go to the NCO club," she said. "Maybe he's hanging out in there."

Rose didn't really believe he was there, and neither did I. She wanted to run into Lance, and she had forgotten that she told me he always went to the club to eat around four in the afternoon, otherwise known as 1600 hours, military time.

I didn't begrudge her that little manipulation. If the tables had been turned and I had a chance to see Harris, even if I had to pretend to help my friend, I would have done it, too. We sat in a strategic location. Right in the center of the big wood paneled room.

Do you come from a land down under?
Where women glow and men plunder?
Can't you hear, can't you hear the thunder?
You'd better run you'd better take cover.

Men at Work blasted from the jukebox while the beat pounded through my stomach. The NCO Club reminded me of one of those dance hall places, grey and shady. Lots of plastic seats and Formica tables like at a roadside truck stop. Not a hint of the tropics in sight. Rose ordered a Margarita and I got a Calamansi juice.

We sat for more than an hour and a half, and if the goal had been to attract attention, it worked.

We both got asked to dance about 137 times and I refused. It has always been against my rules to just dance with anyone who asked. To me, it seemed gross because men being men, they only picked slow songs to dance to anyway. It was like giving them a free pass to grope my body. So I sat alone through several songs, watching Rose, while I held out the hope that, even though I didn't think it would happen, Harris might just walk through the door. At least I reconciled myself to the thought that the more I was out on the base the stronger the likelihood that I would run into him. But this day there was no Lance or Harris and without an alternative scheme we were forced to wait until the next class meeting to find either one.

Next class, Rose was late as usual. Of course, I knew when she finally was ready she would be gorgeous. Always put together with that polished look I envied but could never pull off. I used to watch her change outfits until just the right color combination struck and then she would add shoes and purse to match. Her hair had to be poofed and sprayed to perfection. I couldn't help but feel like a less glamorous stepsister next to her beauty, but at the same time I knew, because the mirror told me so, I wasn't unattractive, myself. Sure, my hair was always a little unruly and I was a bit rounder in the girl parts, but the two of us together out on the town probably looked quite fine to those GIs who were interested in something other than local color.

I waited until five minutes before six, knowing I would get yet another tongue lashing from Asher about being 'disrespectful of the professor and the rest of the class.' Harris had gotten a few of those, too. At least in my case it was Rose's fault not mine, even though I knew I couldn't very well use her as an excuse. I had been calling for at least a half hour and at four minutes 'til, I couldn't take it anymore, so I raced out of the house running as fast as I could down the street to her cul de sac.

After ringing the bell till my finger hurt, I checked the door and walked on in. There was no way she couldn't have heard me.

"Roooooose," I called as I opened the front door. "Hey, are you here? ROSE."

"Wait there, I'm almost done." Her voice had a hollow ring that told me she was in the bathroom.

Unbelievable. She was running this late and still wasn't ready.

I tried to accept the fact that I would be tardy again, and there was nothing to be done about it. Trying to refocus my thoughts, I decided to check out the new bedroom furniture Baby's cousin delivered to Rose the week before.

The sound of the ceiling fan high in the rafters echoed through the huge bedroom. Whoosh, whoosh, whoosh. I still had pangs of envy over the wood floors and spaciousness of the rooms in the barns. The bedspread was meringue white, with a giant yellow gardenia in the center. Drapes to match. I had seen the same design in a catalogue from South Korea. The new furniture was bleached rattan, made to appear French provincial as only a tropical wood could. It was definitely not my taste, but I could see why Rose would like it.

As I walked past the bathroom, I saw the door wide open, so I popped in to see if she was primped to perfection yet. At first, what I saw made me think I was imagining things. But as I looked closer, I took in the complete picture. Rose was sitting on the closed toilet resting a hand with a hypodermic needle in it on one thigh while injecting the needle into a spot on the other thigh.

I backed halfway down the hall and tiptoed the rest of the way to the living room where I sat down as quietly as I could.

"Leah, Leah wait." she called to me from the bathroom. "I'll be out in a minute."

It didn't seem like a minute. And I wasn't even thinking about being late for school anymore. You don't walk in on your best friend shooting up every day.

She wasn't a drug addict. I would have seen the signs. The only other alternative was that that she was sick. But she couldn't be sick because I would have known that, too. I had been with her every day for the past three months. Rose was the picture of health. Almost anyone would want to be in as good a shape as she was.

Nothing made sense.

"Leah, I'm sorry." She pulled up the wicker footstool and sat in front of me. "I know I should have told you."

I braced myself for the explanation not sure of how much honesty I could handle.

"I'm diabetic," she said, waiting for some kind of expression, some look of disgust or fear on my face.

"Jesus Christ, Rose, is that all?" I laughed. "I was scared you were shooting up heroin."

"Soo, yous thought I was a junkie?" She laughed with me. "Now that woulda have been something, I swear you're a Loca."

I shook my head. This time, I agreed with her.

"It was diagnosed when I was seven. Two shots everyday. Like it or not. Soo, I was late today 'cause of JJ's riding lesson, yous know how little kids are. He didn't want to get off the horse, I had to leave the house girl there to deal with him."

I nodded.

On the way to school, without knowing, I ventured into taboo territory.

"You don't act like you're diabetic. You eat ice cream and what about that vodka and the Margaritas? Are you supposed to be doing that?"

"That's why I don't say anything." Rose almost stopped the car in mid-street. "Now yous are gonna act just like my family, tellin' me what I should and shouldn't be doin'."

"Rose, I'm only asking."

"Soo, do yous think I look sick?"

We both knew she didn't, which is why I decided right then and there to keep my mouth shut on the subject of her diabetes.

Soon after, I decided to start driving myself to school. Not because of her illness or even her being late too often, but thanks to Lance. Rose's whereabouts were no longer reliably traceable. She and Lance consummated their relationship and Rose was out of communication more often than not. Lucky for her most of the time Juan was up at Camp John Hay. Anyhow, school nights were prime time for their escapades and I was left without a driver.

Mike had been talking about getting a car for me so that I could go out and do things on my own when he was working. More and more frequently his work took him out of town to bases that were remote, sometimes he even had to drive to the naval base in Illongopo.

After checking the FOR SALE board at the commissary and in the *Philippine Flyer*, the choices were a little, yellow, Toyota and a humongous, white, Chevy Impala. I personally had always wanted a VW convertible so I voted for the Toyota, but the 1973 Chevy worked better, even if it was the size and weight of a small tank. I didn't complain. It got me around. With its white-on-black interior and from just the mere size of the thing, it looked more like a boat than a car.

I was happy driving around in the boat because in a place like Clark, wheels meant freedom. But I knew where I wanted to go and I knew it was wrong of me to pick up another man in a car bought by my husband.

Chapter 8

In mid-February, Asher planned for us to have an outdoor meeting. More accurately, he had just gone along with what everyone else wanted. By the fourth week of class we had suffered enough of the stuffiness in the high school science lab. My clothes always smelled of formaldehyde and even more so when he brought the jars filled with a human heart and lungs. You could say we sort of forced him to make the next session an outdoor potluck just so that we could get outside and breathe. It was perfect picnic weather. Not as blistering hot as it is in August or even October. In February, the Philippine Islands were almost pleasant. I loved weather like that. It had a back home kind of feel. Not that I ever wanted to go back home, but I had to admit something familiar was nice for a change.

My energy soared, as did my spirits. I wore a light jacket and my favorite jeans fit perfectly that day. They didn't make me sweat either, so I could wear them without having denim sticking to my rear. When I dressed for school that evening, I knew I looked good, and looking good had become so terribly important.

Asher found a shady spot under a spreading mimosa tree next to the high school. I knew that spot well. I sometimes went there even on days when I had no class. One of my favorite haunts on base. I would sit under that tree and imagine myself living on the emerald green hill that dominated the landscape. Many times I considered painting it, but I never did. In my world, it was a magical place where dreams should come true.

Most of the guys in the class lived in the dorm, so they ate in the chow hall. Not exactly a place to order dishes suited for pot luck, which explains why we had six Chicken Coop buckets, and four pizzas from the Airman's Club. Lucy surprised me by her ability to cook after all, and thanks to her, I brought some banana lumpia and pancit bihon. It was the only Filipino food at the picnic.

Asher brought his wife, Pitpong, who had just arrived from Thailand. She made this God-awful smelling stuff full of Chinese rice noodles. Since I couldn't get past the smell, and I was afraid of what it contained, I didn't bother to try it.

Unlike like most other GIs, I could tell Harris had manners. They heaped large mountains of pizza, chicken, potato chips, pancit and that nasty smelling Thai stuff on their plates. I waited for the soggy paper to cave under the weight of all the food, but they bolted it all down with San Miguel beer so fast it never had a chance to wilt.

Harris took only the amount he knew he could, or should eat. He only ate the white meat of the chicken, first peeling the crusty coating off, and passing up the pepperoni pizza for a slice with only cheese. He didn't seem to like potato chips, but nachos with Jalapeños were definitely a yes. Like me, he vetoed the Thai stuff, and based on that act, again, I was renewed in my decision that fate had been kind. I had found my soul mate

Nobody really wanted to study the endocrine system while cramming themselves with greasy chicken legs, but this day couldn't be wasted. If I were planning to take up the challenge and do something about Harris, I would have to do it soon. There were only four more weeks of class and then, who knew? We might be separated forever. No chance to talk. Maybe only to cross paths occasionally at the Bobbitt Theater or the NCO Club by chance. I couldn't let the evening pass without making a move. I began masterminding a plan of attack.

Around 2000 hours, the sky started to darken. Not so dark that you couldn't see in front of you, but certainly dark enough that it was impossible to have any semblance of a class session. We had a choice to take it inside or dismiss early. Dismissing won out, of course.

That's when I panicked. Until that point I had only said, "Hi," to Harris the whole evening. There was no way now to open the conversation. He looked like he was gearing up to get on his bike and ride off into the sunset when I just blurted out.

"Want a ride?"

HELLO.

EARTH TO LEAH.

The man had a ride.

What the hell did I think that thing with two wheels and a handlebar was? What an idiotic question. He stared at me as if he was trying to decide what to do.

"Can I put the bike in your trunk?" Okay, maybe it wasn't such a stupid question after all.

"Sure," I said. My heart sounded like it was having its own drum brigade. I could hardly believe he was going to be sitting in the car with me in less than five minutes.

Thank God for the 73 Chevy Impala. Harris's bike fit in perfectly, but to keep the lid closed, we had to use a rope. I had one of Jessie's old jump ropes stashed under the spare tire.

He took the rope, expertly wound it through the latch, and secured the lid. I watched in awe, but then I was in awe and wonder at anything he did. When he gave me back the car keys his hand lightly brushed against mine. My senses alerted to the current that ran from my hand to my toes.

"Where do you live?" I asked. Now I would get the information that I needed to scope out his whereabouts on those off days when there was no school.

Before he could answer though, I had a deep knowing. I sometimes call it an intuitional hit. I've had it more than once in my life. Sort of a feeling that I know what will happen before it occurs. I sensed that the information about where he lived would be irrelevant, and that from that night on, for quite a while, I would only have to look to my side to find him.

He didn't seem to mind my mild interrogations. I asked him benign questions, and he never hedged or seemed uncomfortable about telling me where he lived or worked, or even the fact that he wrote poetry in his spare time.

When it was his turn to do the asking, he spared me no such courtesies.

"How long have you been married? Are you happy? Why not? Are you going to leave him?"

We had rounded the corner near the Mabuhay Café, when he finally made it clear where he wanted the night to go. "I'm not really an early sleeper, would you like to get some coffee and talk for a while?"

I had been hoping he would ask. It was either going to be me, or him, and to my relief at least I was spared the humiliation of having to do the asking.

The café was full of military types in their fatigues. They always seemed to favor their green fatigues over the dress blues. I guess it really depended on what job one had. A 702 office worker wouldn't wear fatigues any more than an airplane mechanic would wear a starched blue uniform every day.

The booth had a torn pleather seat, the kind that makes half a circle. I was glad he didn't take me to one of those clubs on base where the skinny little girls from the Odyssey did table dances. At least the atmosphere at the Mabuhay was more intimate, like a campus coffee shop at Ohio State. He got up and ordered without asking me, and he returned with two bottles of San Miguel and two lemon sodas.

"I thought you were getting coffee?" I asked.

"I changed my mind. Besides, I knew you liked lemonade." The smile lingered on his face longer than I expected. "This is my specialty. Try it." I watched curiously as he poured half beer and half lemon soda into the glasses.

"It's a remnant of my days in Madrid. *Cerveza con limón.*"

Even from only my high school Spanish, I could tell his Castilian accent was perfect.

He handed me the glass. "Are you tired?"

I shook my head.

"Good, then let's make this toast to awakenings."

With that we clinked our glasses and Harris cheered, "*Salud.*"

"Now," he said as he relaxed into his seat, "tell me everything about you. All about your life."

It sounded like a tall order, but two *cerveza con limons* later, I had spilled out most of the highlights of my perfectly ordinary 29 years and had topped it off with how I had never been in love with the man I had married.

"Is that why you're here with me?" Harris asked.

Once again, without even thinking, I answered him.

"Yes."

We could have easily walked it. But the bike was still peeking out the trunk and I was driving him home in the boat. Night on Clark Air Base was balmy and fresh. It held the scent of magnolia and jasmine. The street in front of Meyer's hall was lined with more mimosas. I don't think most people stationed at Clark realized it, but it truly was a paradise.

Chapter 9

Entering another person's private space is intrusive. Even when they allow you to be there, you are moving about their inner sanctum. The mere fact of crossing that threshold gave me a chill. I knew regardless of what would happen or not happen, Harris and I were creating a story and this was its true beginning.

On the wall opposite the door was some white paper with a handwritten quotation:

The meeting of two personalities is like the contact of two chemical substances, if there is any reaction, both are transformed. ~Rollo May

My mother always said the condition of your room reflects the condition of your mind. Needless to say, this was mostly preached to me on those days when my room closely resembled an obstacle course in an ammunitions dump.

Harris's mind was not exactly cluttered, but it didn't work like an IBM mainframe, either. He definitely favored the color blue. Okay, true, I already knew that, but the room confirmed it. His faded blue terrycloth robe was thrown over the round Papasan chair and a blue bedspread covered the twin-sized bed.

He flipped the switch on the Sony boom box that dominated his bedside table. While he fiddled about the room, I took it all in. He wore contact lens. The case, a pair of glasses, *Love and Will* By Rollo May, a bowl of incense, two ball point pens, a GI issue table lamp and a couple of opened letters cluttered the table on the other side of his bed.

He liked music. Three boxes of albums sat on the floor near the wardrobe. Air Supply, Journey and Toto were at the top of each pile. He had traveled. Posters of Australia, India, Panama and Spain covered the walls. I suppose some of them could have been on a wish list, but I knew he had been to Spain so I figured he had visited the rest as well.

He hung the bike on the wall. On one of those special hooks that he had put there to hold it. He dug through the multitude of books that covered every shelf and pulled two from the group then sat on the bed. I stood in the corner of the room watching.

"Come here, sit." He motioned to me, tapping the area of the bed beside him. "I want to show you something."

What he wanted me to see were the volumes of his poetry.

With music barely playing in the background, he read each one slowly, emphasizing the words that carried meaning. I felt myself drift away, taken up to dreamland by a voice that hovered in space, lilting and cooing me from nervousness to calm like the sound of a mother's lullaby.

He didn't rest between pages. His lyrics went on. His voice was soft. I felt as if he had written the words only for me and I was transported. When he finished he asked, "What do you think?"

"They're beautiful," I said, because they were.

"You're beautiful," He replied. Taking my face in his hands, he kissed my forehead first, then my lips.

Moments like that are only meant to be lived, not talked about. Moments when you find your heart pouring open, leaping from your chest, melting and dripping, oozing and enveloping you, then falling into that other person. The only person in the world who could possibly share a moment like that with you. I could hear a man named Franks singing about a Tahitian Moon. Through the curtains I could see the dark of Philippine sky, but lying next to Harris that night, my soul beat in time with the heart of every star-crossed lover who had ever lived.

Morning found me in my bed at home,

languishing in disbelief at what had occurred the night before. When I left Harris, it was still dark out, but the musings of dawn had begun. Sneaking back into a house that I called my own felt strange. I had flashbacks of my teen years, when I tried to scurry to bed after a too long, but quite innocent night out, praying that my parents would be none the wiser.

My fears that night were needless. Never mind that we usually slept in separate rooms anyway, Michael had been called to John Hay while I was at class, so the only one who might figure out I had spent the night somewhere else was Lucy. I didn't worry about her because by now she was almost an accessory after the fact. Not that I had discussed Harris with her, but she was always in the room when Rose and I were talking. She would have had to be a turnip not to notice the less than subtle hints about our comings and goings.

I had grown to love my brand new ranch style home on the base. It was cozy. No matter where we lived, or what was going in our lives, I was good at decorating a house. I can say that without being boastful, because it was simply a fact. Almost everyone who came into my house talked about how nice it looked. I took a lot of pride in my decorating, because it's well known that I am not the housekeeping type, and as far as cooking is concerned, well, other than to make a quick lunch or dinner, it always seemed like such a waste. You make a beautiful dish, take hours to prepare it and in less than twenty minutes the whole thing is gone. Much like the Tibetan mandalas. I read how the monks take so much time and effort to create these fantastic pictures with sand, for hours and hours they work, then swoosh, in one second someone takes a rake and wipes it all away. It's supposed to teach them impermanence. Nothing in this world lasts forever.

But as much as I loved it, the morning after being with Harris, my house was a lonely shell. I climbed into bed still drunk from either *cerveza con limón*, or something less tangible. My double bed had grown exponentially and there was nowhere to go to get away from the chill of the island heat. I piled comforters over and around me, searching for warmth. Curling up into a fetus only made me feel aborted. My mind and body searching for home, both felt foreign. I thought of taking a bath to relax. Usually, the warm suds were my sure cure for insomnia, but the idea of washing Harris away jolted me. I placed my hands over my face and took in a deep breath. He was still with me. The scent of my skin soothed the nerves and I drifted off with the memory of his face on mine.

Chapter 10

"Jesus Christ woman, where the hell have you been?" yelled Rose.

She was standing in my doorway decked out in her Sunday best.

"What time is it?" I mumbled with one eye open.

"It's 1:30 in the AFTERNOON and WHERE WERE YOU last night? I looked everywhere. I even drove over to the Airmen's Club. Did you even GO to school?"

I could hear Lucy and the girls outside playing in the front yard.

"What time did you say it was?" I asked, hoping I hadn't heard correctly.

She shoved the watch in my face. "Geez I've got to get up. I am supposed to meet Harris at two."

"Uhhuh, uhhuh."

She stopped me as I moved to stand. "Wait just a minute Loca–you're holdin' out on me."

Lightly pushing me against the bed with her newly manicured hand, I had no choice but to sink back into the covers.

"You were with Harris all night weren't yous?... OH MY GOD. You were. No fucking way. I want details."

"I don't have time right now Rose. I have to get dressed."

She pushed me back as I tried to move. "No, no, no, yous aren't getting' outta here without givin' me some details."

There was no point trying to deny Rose when she got like this.

"Fine," I said, "but let me get up and get ready."

I gave her the PG rated version of what had transpired the night before, all the way up to the kiss. And then she shot me one of her looks.

"And...?"

"And what?" I answered, knowing perfectly well what she was waiting for.

"Loca, I know you. If yous aren't tellin' there's somethin' to tell. Anyhow I already knew it. When I couldn't find you I told Lance that you had gotten hold of Harris and you weren't about to let him go. So, what was he like?"

"You told Lance?" The implications of that statement struck me. I didn't like the idea of her telling people about my situation with Mike or

Harris or even talking about me at all.

She had all the gossip from me that she was getting for the time being. I was in a big hurry to get over to the Kelly Cafeteria where I was due in less than ten minutes thanks to Rose and her insistence on hearing "details."

At 1403, I waited outside of the cafeteria for Harris to arrive. All over Clark Air Base were these American looking buildings that reminded me I was only halfway in another country. Of course, I was planted smack dab in the middle of Luzon Island, in the Philippines, but, to be honest, it wasn't until I ventured outside the gates of the base that I really felt like I was in a foreign land. The US government had everything on base sanitized and totally American. Kelly Cafeteria was one of those places. To my mind, it would have been a whole lot more interesting if they had gone with the local architecture and really played up the exotic look.

I leaned my shoulder against the brick wall that surrounded three sides of the cafeteria and occupied myself by listening to the conversations of the women who walked by. They were knee deep in discussion about potted plants and bougainvillea. It was making my brain soft. I sometimes wondered how I ended up in a woman's body when I hated women's talk. It always seemed so trivial. Talk about babies, and Tupperware, plants and purses. Not heady stuff for sure. Not the kind of thing Harris would talk with me about on a lazy afternoon. I knew that much about him already.

At 1412, I wondered if he would show up. Snippets of my Catholic upbringing lingered, and I envisioned Sister Francis Joan at the podium warning us girls, "If you sin and give in to a boy, he will never respect you. He probably will never even call you again. Once a boy gets what he wants from you, he is finished."

It was the old, 'why buy the cow if you can have the milk for free?' argument.

But what if she was right?

I mentally said: Erase.

What happened the night before was bigger than sex, and it wasn't something that either of us was going to walk away from so easily. I was certain.

Almost.

Harris walked up behind me and tapped me on the shoulder. He was wearing that blue shirt, the one that he wore with the sleeves rolled up. He was as handsome a man as I had ever seen.

"Sorry I'm late. I got a ride with some friends. They're over at the car. I want you to meet them."

He already wanted me to meet his friends. It meant that he was planning to be with me for more than just a night.

So much for Sister Francis Joan.

If I had been back in Columbus and not on an air base, I would have sworn I'd seen Alex at the Kismet dancing the night away with my friend, Phillip. In fact, Alex would have been exactly Phillip's type. He had a beautiful face, not a strong one. Denise, on the other hand, looked far more the male. An odd pairing, but one I had seen many times before in the Air Force. And unlike a lot of folks around military installations, I was fine with it. I always felt it was a shame that the US military had their stupid policy. I couldn't for the life of me figure out what one's sexual orientation had to do with the ability to carry a gun or change a tire on a jeep.

Harris and I sat stoically in the back seat of their car. We glanced at each other and smiled.

"We need to stop and get some Pampers. Do you mind?" Alex asked.

I didn't mind anything as long as Harris was with me.

We waited in the car while they went into the BX. I'm sure they both didn't need to go on the diaper mission, but I sensed they were giving us some alone time and it was appreciated.

Harris spoke first. "Leah, are you okay about last night?" When he used my name for the first time, my stomach sank. He took my hand and held on tight.

"I love you," I said.

I had done it again.

Normally, in human interactions there is that sensor. You put it on your mouth until you process the thoughts you are about to let out. In other words, every stupid thing that drops from the brain into the area of the lips should not be said out loud. My filter had lost its ability to work when I was around Harris. Everything just came bolting through. I felt like I was speaking another language. One I didn't understand too well.

Waiting to see how he would respond was ten-second torture.

Tick, tick, tick.

I stiffened while I anticipated his lack of response. I tried not to worry, but I did, because once I had thrown it into the universe, I couldn't very well take it back. Even if I had wanted to. My only thought was, *What in the world will he think of me, blurting out declarations of love after what was nothing more than a one-night stand?*

Tick,tick,tick.

I held my breath. He took my other hand in his and kissed me softly.

Tick, tick, tick.

"Me too, you," he whispered.

We spent an hour or so with Alex and Denise at their house. Naturally, they lived in a barn. Only they appreciated it. Alex had collected these bizarre tribal hats he picked up flying F16s over the Pacific theater. While Denise was putting the boys down for a nap, he was happy to take us to the bedroom where he had arranged the hats on the wall over the bed. He built the bed, himself, made of concrete blocks and wood slats with a mattress on top.

After a few minutes, Alex remembered some unfinished business in the shed behind the barn and dashed off to leave the two of us standing alone. I hoped it had not been too obvious that I only wanted to be with Harris, but we had had so little time since the past evening in his room, I was craving just him. Not friends, not conversation, not a day of pleasantries.

When the door closed, Harris leaned in to hug me. "You about ready to go?," he asked, reading my face.

I nodded.

"Let's just say our goodbyes and then head over to my dorm, okay?"

The rest of the day we spent in his room listening to Journey and ordering delivery from the Pizza Palace. The hours were slow and languid as we heard the daylight activities continue on outside. For us though, day and night didn't exist. Heaven on Earth was room 310 in Meyer's Hall on Clark Air Base, Angeles City, island of Luzon in the country of the Philippines.

Chapter 11

The next evening, when class began, Harris had retired his bicycle and I moved to the opposite side of the room to sit behind him.

If you think a move like that went unnoticed, think again. Poor Dr. Asher had no chance. His dry delivery on the functions of the adrenal glands was in direct competition with the two of us, and the winners hands down, belonged to the new couple instead of the overhead.

I tried to look solemn enough to hide the giddiness bubbling just beneath the surface. Harris, attempting to be clever in his delivery, reached behind to hand me a note. I was in junior high school all over again. Thoughts of Eddie, the tangle haired boy that I obsessed over in 7th grade took hold, and I recalled how even though I thought Eddie was cute, I knew he wasn't the one, because his name wasn't Michael.

I looked up after reading, *Meet me at the tree,* to find thirteen pairs of eyes, including a bespeckled set belonging to Asher, beamed towards my direction. Anonymity on an air base like Clark was next to impossible. There were 35,000 people living there, and for some reason instead of rotating clockwise around the entire population, you were more likely to see the same 350 over and over and over again. The odd thing is that even though I didn't know the other 34,650 from you know who, any one of them might have had top-secret information about my intimate associations. At that point, I should have thought about the consequences of my actions and of Mike, the husband, but the truth is, I didn't.

As soon as Asher called for that twenty-minute break, I dashed to the mimosa. Memories of our times together in the past few days swirled around my head, and when Harris arrived a minute later trying to be discreet, I was smitten all over again.

Evenings in the PI glow from light cast only the way a tropical sunset can. The color is deeper than a sunset in North America, and on that night, the sky had turned one of my favorite shades of magenta. The grass was lush and cushiony beneath my feet, and as soon as I touched it, I flung off my sandals so I could dig my toes down to feel the coolness of the ground below. Harris leaned against the tree and pulled me in.

"I've been waiting for one hour and...," he looked intently at his watch, "...43 minutes, to do this."

Like most women, I had been kissed by a few men. I hadn't kept count, but it was probably more than ten and less than twenty. So I had the theory that the kiss would tell it all.

Maybe I was a victim of too many movies.

You kiss the guy, fireworks happen, your shoes fall off, things of that nature. My shoes were already off so I didn't worry about that part. But when Harris kissed me again I should have lost consciousness. My insides rolled. Not from the fireworks that you always hear about, but roller coasters, Ferris wheels, the merry-go-round all in one. It was joy and pain. Pleasure and torment. We kissed for a long time and then tears came to my eyes. He saw them and dabbed with his little finger.

"I'm afraid," I whispered.

"Because it's so strong?"

So he felt it, too.

"Let it be, Leah," he said. "This only happens once in a lifetime."

He didn't seem to have the fear I had, but fear and all, I no longer had a choice. The something I feared had already happened, and I was helpless to control it. He had brought me to a place I had dreamt of all my life, so I let him lead me deeper.

When I was at home, the outside world and Harris couldn't exist. I was a mother and even though Mike and I were not getting along, I was still his wife.

Jessie begged me for gymnastics lessons and since she had taken to using that non-functioning water pump as a pummel horse it was certainly better to channel her talent into a real activity.

"They have lessons at the base gym," she said. Then, using her best sales technique, she added, "And they're cheap."

Of course, I wasn't going to be the one paying for things like gymnastics from my pittance of an allowance, so I returned with the standard reply of, "Go ask your father."

She was overjoyed when he told her she could start the very next week. I was relieved too, because it meant she had a place to let out all of that energy and motion. There was less likelihood of losing an arm or leg in a supervised setting.

Dana wasn't interested in things like gymnastics yet. Besides, she and Lucy were having a blast hanging out at the playground around the corner.

Lucy came to me one day and said Dana had been, "Tuffing poods." I had no idea what that meant. It sounded ridiculous to my ear, and as bad as her English was I had no way to even translate the phrase. In frustration, she took me to Dana's room and pointed under her bed.

Spread like a picnic on a summer day, was a private stash of bananas, mangoes, and a whole pitcher of Kool-Aid. The pitcher was so big I couldn't figure out how she moved it from the fridge to her room, without spilling all over the floor. Did she think a war was coming and the commissary would close? The child had never starved a day in her life, but she continued to put food under her bed the entire time we lived at that house. When I finally asked her why she did it, she told me it was "just in case."

Mike, the husband, was still oblivious to my pastime activities. He always had been. He was preoccupied with work as usual, and in the snatches of time that he spent at home, he amused himself with his prize possession, the stereo. He had created it with love from separate components he picked up on junkets to Japan and Korea. There were woofers and tweeters and equalizers. And speakers. Oh, so many speakers. The two smaller ones were mounted on walls, and the other four sat in each corner of the room. Personally, I didn't understand his fascination with the "sound system" as he called it. It vibrated the floors in the house and shook all the pictures, but as long as he kept it in his private space, I could handle it. I did feel sorry for Lucy and the girls since they slept on his side of the house.

Despite the fact that things were working, I had an overwhelming, but not very wise desire to tell Mike about Harris. Clandestine meetings in dark corners were not part of who I wanted to be. Up until then, the one thing I had done right in the marriage was being faithful.

Most of the time, before Harris, my discussions with Mike were more about how unhappy I was and how I wanted to leave him. Never had a conversation begun with, "I have met someone else." But I knew if I had a talk with Mike this time that would certainly be the opening line. Common sense told me disclosure was neither a smart idea, nor was it necessary right away. We had lots of time before us in the PI, and it would be best to keep things as they were, if possible. It was the prudent thing to do. Later, we could figure out the details without making things messy.

I told Harris that in my own brand of logic, living with Mike felt like I was being unfaithful. Not to Mike, but to him. I felt like I was cheating on Harris by even sharing the same space with a man I never really loved. Once in a great while, I was called upon to do my wifely duty and more and more frequently, when I was with my husband I became nauseous.

All the times I decided to leave Mike, I eventually backed down because of the fear I wouldn't be able to take care of Dana and Jessie on my own. But a marriage shouldn't be based on fear, so as much as I prided myself on being honest, I was living a whopper of a lie. There was not enough love to make a partnership, but too many obligations and too much history to dissolve it.

I had the kids and Harris had to work on the aircraft , so on Mondays and Wednesdays, I would stay with him as late as I could without causing suspicion. I know most men would kill if they had a wife out half the night, but not Mike. I knew then, what I had always felt, we really were nothing but roommates.

The car worked well for the rest of the semester and half of the next, until one day, my boat finally and permanently docked. It had been slowing down and I had the notion it wouldn't be long before it either sank or hit sand. First, there was a ping here and a bing there, and then some God awful grinding noise that followed. Sure enough, my trusty old Chevy lost its battle. It was relegated to the spare parts brigade and I was forced to rely on Padi Ko Taxi for transportation. But not even a sunken ship stopped my planned evenings with Harris. Sometimes we took the base bus outside the gates after school and then went out to the jazz clubs on MacArthur Highway. Or we found out-of-the-way coffee houses and sat for hours just being in each other's company. Other nights, we strolled along the small streets that dotted Plaridels I and II, or the base parade grounds. But of course, there were also nights when we just wanted to be alone in room 310.

Wednesdays were our talking nights. Harris liked the routine. On those nights, discussions were often serious and probing. The dark balmy air was perfect for sitting on rocks in the field behind my house. Or on top of Signal Hill near the elementary school. To me, the moon in the PI seemed to be extraordinarily bright that year. I thought it was my imagination, but Harris said he believed in his heart that the chemistry of love changed everything in its vicinity. So to think that the moon would respond to our desire was not an idea so out of reach. When he spoke like that, it was as if I had wasted all the years of my life on trivial matters. Things like my weight and hairstyles, or what someone said about me to hurt my feelings didn't matter anymore. My anger at growing up in a place where I never felt I belonged disappeared. Harris's world was full of ideas, hypothesizes, theories and philosophy so thick I could cut it like layer cake and devour its sweetness. Mine, until I met him, was mundane and full of confusion and misconnections. But as we spent more time together, I felt our kindred spirits bloom in each other's presence. I started to become who I had aspired to be all along. Funny, I had always thought of myself as smart. I had graduated from high school as an honor student. I guess that made me feel like I knew at least a little about a lot of things. But knowing Harris expanded my thinking more than any class or lecture ever had. Being in love had proven to be the real teacher.

As we lay on a blanket atop Signal Hill, an idea came to me. When I told him, he hugged me so hard I thought I would lose my breath. The tears I had cried before were then his.

I said to him, in a quiet voice, more sure of myself than I had ever been before, "I think there must be this magical moment, when two minds and hearts connect on a level that can't be measured. That is when you know something greater exists. And from that point on, it's like being able to glimpse into another world."

No one on Clark Air Base that year could see when that magic occurred in Harris and me. I can tell you though. Because it was true that love, in its ability to transform, took us away from the normal and into the realm of the extraordinary. When I see movies that remind me, or songs that declare it, I remember how I changed from a regular person into a person who could touch her own soul.

On the night of the 1982 earthquake, a 6.2 whooper, we sat in Montez Park near the Pizza Palace. He handed me a book called, *The Autobiography of a Yogi,* and said, "If you never read another book in your entire life, you must read this."

From the picture of the man with long flowing hair inside the front cover, I had a sense of how important it might be. But back then, I of course didn't know the part it would play later in my life.

I leafed through the pages and as if on cue, the earth shook. From the startled look I gave, Harris could see I was spooked.

"Synchronicity," he chuckled.

It was a word that would come up more and more often in my thoughts from that day on.

The ancients say there is a sympathy of all things. The entire universe works together to create this synchronicity. When like minds come together in love they can only create the highest good. We are all part of the same consciousness, but working under a spell that we are separate. It took a blending of the minds, or in this case, a blending of two hearts, to help me know what this meant. There are no coincidences. There was no coincidence in our meeting.

If I think back to how it happened, me from Ohio, him born in Spain, over the seas, sharing this same small piece of earth, at the same moment in time, there must be a purpose. I had to wonder why I really made this journey. More and more I started to see that staying with Mike was the only way this could have come to pass. In my heart there was such sadness about that. I used a relationship that I didn't want to open the door for a love that would never fade. I think I knew it when I agreed to come. That tingling inside was telling me I had to follow my heart. And if it brought me to this point, then I know it brought me home.

Chapter 12

For several weeks, I saw Rose at school, but that was all. Just as I was about to write her off, one Sunday morning she called and suggested we eat brunch together at the Officers' Club. I missed hanging out with Rose and all of her wildness, leading me into temptation. The house girls shared a table with the kids, so we could turn talk to the one subject we shared. It was no secret that Juan went on maneuvers to Camp John Hay at least two weeks out of the month, which made Rose a free agent. I was jealous. She didn't have to hide or spend hours in a dorm room just to be with Lance. She had him over to her place most of the time.

"Has he meet JJ yet?," I asked.

"Yeah about a week ago," she said.

"Aren't you worried JJ will tell his dad?"

"Naw. He's in bed by seven." She sounded confident. "Plus I told him that Uncle Lance was Mommy's imaginary friend. So even if he does say something it's gonna sound all loco and Juan won't believe him. You remember when JJ had all those imaginary friends he talked about a couple of months ago? Juan will just think he has started all that mess up again."

"Yeah but Rose, this imaginary friend is a grown man. And don't forget he is visible." I couldn't help but think this was her most hair brained scheme ever.

"What if something happened and Juan came home unexpectedly? What if he found Lance there?" I continued.

"I'm gonna tell him, Leah. I'm gonna leave." She said it with no expression whatsoever.

"You mean now?" I jumped. "You mean leave the Philippines and everything?"

She shook her head. She was close to tears. It was not a look I had ever seen on Rose's face.

"I have to."

"Oh God, Rose you're not...?"

"Don't be stupid Loca."

"Okay then, I don't get it. What about the ten year plan?"

"Things are just happening faster than I thought," she answered.

"Lance has orders to Kadena. He leaves in two months."

"So?" I knew if she felt half of what I was feeling for Harris this seemed like the end of the world, but…

"Can't you just meet like once a month? Okinawa isn't that far away. You can take the $10.00 hop. I'd even go with you once or twice."

"It's not that simple. I just need to be with Lance." She insisted.

I could tell she had made up her mind.

"You haven't even told Juan."

I didn't know where to go from that point.

"I'm flying to the Dominican Republic to get the divorce. It's the closest place to home and it only takes a day. Then when I get to Puerto Rico I'll wait for Lance. He's gonna come there to get me and we'll get married before we leave."

"Rose, it's too soon. You've only known him a few months."

"Soo you've only known Harris a few months. How long did it take you to know?"

I sat in silence. I didn't want her to go, and yet, I wanted her to have the happy ending I dreamed of, too.

I smiled at her and said, "I am so damn jealous of you right now."

But, I could see a vulnerability in Rose's eyes that I hadn't noticed before. I didn't ask and she didn't tell, but we both knew there was more to the story.

"You know what?" She turned on a dime.

"We oughta get outta here for reals. I mean off this piece of shit air force base. You know, yous, me, Lance and Harris? We need a break. Too many eyes in this place, I'm sick of lookin at em."

Harris suggested Baguio because it was cold and mountainous. A breath of fresh air, away from the center of our mosquito infested island. He told me once how much he loved the Pyrenees in Spain, and in India the breezes that blew across the foothills of the Himalayas. But I had forgotten that Camp John Hay was close by and that it was Juan's home away from Clark.

The bus pulled up in front of The Oriental Hotel. A lot was left wanting in the name and décor, but the hotel was located on Magsaysay Street, and that meant we would be nestled up against the green hills of Baguio. I found an ad for it in the tourist book I kept stashed in the back of my closet. Until then I hadn't been anywhere more than a mile from Clark, so I had little use for it. I didn't know it at the time, but that little book had earned a reputation as a travel guide for the bored, but very married, women who were having affairs with enlisted men or locals.

After dinner with Rose and Lance at the Orchid Bar, Harris and I went off on our own and took a walk through the city. I was happy to be amongst real people for a change. Not just the military, but Filipino families. People with real lives. No bar girls and no GIs. We spent a lot of time that night strolling along the edge of the lagoon at Burnham Park. We watched children on horseback and other couples nuzzling under the weeping willows. As much as Harris loved the mountains, I loved the water. Being next to water I felt content. He could see the way it changed me.

"We should live by the water," he said. "Someday we will have a house in the mountains, by a lake…where I can write and you can paint."

I was feeling luckier by the minute and not so envious of Rose anymore. Maybe this wasn't just a PI romance after all. Maybe it was a lasting love. I had cried many tears already, hoping that someday we would have a forever, but I had to keep those thoughts at bay. I was always so afraid to think that far ahead. Afraid to jinx it.

As much as I had wanted to ask him what he thought we would be to each other after the Philippines, I knew I didn't have the right. I was the one who wasn't free.

We sat on one of the benches and he told me how his parents divorced. How bad it was for him and his brother.

"I wanted to die when my dad left," he said. "I hated my mom for it too."

"Do you know why?" I asked.

"I think maybe it was the Korean War still in his blood. It did something to him, that war. I don't know what, because he never talked about it."

"What about your mom?"

"First she took us back to Spain to be with her family, but then she thought we would have a better life in the states. So we moved there. We stayed in Seattle for a couple of years, and then Virginia, but by the time I graduated from high school we had moved again, to Colorado."

"I know it seemed bad to you," I told him, "but I would have given anything to have lived in different countries and states."

"I was lost, you know? I had no anchor. We never stayed anywhere long enough to have a real home. My dad's family had their home in Kansas, and my mom's in Granada, but I had no place to be from. I need a place to call home, Leah."

All the talk about divorce made the guilt in me rise, but even still, more than anything in the world I wanted to be that home.

Before we headed back to our room, Harris told me how he fell in love with me the first day of Anatomy 101. He told it as if I hadn't been there, going over every detail, what I wore, and how many times I glanced in his direction. He had memorized the lines of my face, which he called apple shaped, and he almost whispered as he admitted that when he closed his eyes to sleep that first night, he tried to imagine me next to him. He said he thought I had to be married, because I didn't seem like the Air Force type. And he said he thought that life in its cruelty had brought him to a love that couldn't be his, but couldn't be denied, either.

Twirling my curls through his fingers, he promised he would never love another woman as much as he loved me right then. He told me we were chosen. I believed him when he said that God, whoever He, She, or It was, had looked down upon our two separate, pathetic souls and given us the chance in this life to feel the true strength and power of love that Heloise and Abelard, Romeo and Juliet, Anthony and Cleopatra had known.

He speculated that not many humans had the depth to feel this much emotion. I suspected it was the truth.

Passion that I had wanted so desperately when I married, but had never experienced, was mine that night with Harris. I was more married to him in those moments than I had ever been to Mike. It occurred to me that marriage in the eyes of our creator was a binding declaration of love and devotion, one that came from the heart, and not an ink splattered piece of paper that bore the great seal from the state of Ohio.

Chapter 13

By the time we returned home, word was out that one of Juan's buddies had seen Rose with a guy in Baguio. She didn't deny it. She simply said it was better this way. Since she had planned to tell him she was leaving, at least the ice was broken.

Juan came flying home from John Hay in a rage and Rose didn't call me for three days. She didn't go to school on Monday night, and I was starting to fear for her safety. As a rule, military men, I guess any men really, didn't take well to having it known that their wives were having affairs. From what I knew about Juan, he wasn't going to be the exception.

So when Rose stood at my door on Tuesday looking like a lost little puppy, I put my arms around her, hugged her, and showed her to the sofa.

"He knows everything." She said after she had a chance to sit and calm herself.

I was already privy to that bit of information. But to make it official, I guess she had to declare it.

"What did he say, Rose?"

"Nothing," she whispered.

I gave her a look of disbelief and she could see I wasn't buying the spin she had put on it.

"He said he knew it would happen one day, and he didn't have any hard feelings. He just told me to make arrangements to leave as soon as possible. Said it looks bad for an officer to have his wife running around with an enlisted man."

This was a fact even I couldn't deny.

I couldn't believe my ears. "You mean he doesn't care?"

"I didn't say he doesn't care," she declared through the tears, "it's just that he knows we haven't been good for such a long time, and you can't go on like that forever."

"So when are you going?"

"End of next month. Lance will have his thirty-day leave. He can fly over with me."

Just like that. All settled. Problem solved.

The Philippines had done for my marriage what no place else had been able to do. It turned us into two completely separate entities co-existing in the same house but never crossing paths. I had no doubt that there were nights when Mike wondered where I was. He was either afraid to find out the truth, or just happy that I had stopped bitching about the lack of love in our relationship. Whichever it was, it was working to help me go along blindly maintaining the status quo. Nothing was forcing me to stir up the sludge at the bottom.

Harris and I had begun to finish each other's sentences and anticipate the other's needs. When I remembered all those self-help books saying you have to work at a relationship to keep it going, I thought of Mike. That is exactly what I had done. I had worked. And worked. And continued to work, and what had come of it but unhappiness and frustration. I believed the kind of relationship people are searching for was the one I had with Harris, not work but easy, open and fluid.

Once I had a conversation with my mother about things like getting married. I asked her how I would know when I met the one person that was right for me. I have never forgotten her answer, "You'll just know."

I was convinced her advice would never do me much good. I thought I knew when I met Mike. Of course, we all know how well that turned out.

So I had lost faith in her words. Until Harris. Now that I know it can happen in a second, and if one of my girls asked me the same question, I would probably have the same answer.

I know my parents loved each other, but since I had never seen two people as much in love as we were, including even Rose and Lance, I was certain they didn't know what I was experiencing with Harris. Even after I started looking, I didn't see it in other people. Sometimes I would point out a couple and ask Harris if he thought they were feeling what we felt.

He would always answer the same way. "I think we were chosen," or "What we have is special."

Sometimes it felt as if we lived above Earth.

In the midst of the monsoon rains, one afternoon Harris shook me from my comfort and disturbed me so deeply I feared I would never recover. We were in his room. Right after making love. Journey's "Open Arms" played on the stereo and I had wrapped myself in the blue terrycloth robe.

Harris had been solemn that day. More into his private thoughts than usual. I couldn't reach him the way I normally did.

Eventually he told me about a dream.

"I saw myself running from a bear. He was huge, and dark, with disgusting features, and the faster I ran the closer he got. As he came closer I could see you in the distance. You were calling for me and telling me to come with you, but I couldn't reach. I kept running towards you but he was catching up with me. The closer he got, the farther you were, until you faded and I had the feeling that he swallowed me whole."

Harris loved Carl Jung and books on the meaning of dreams, so I knew this would bother him for days. I stroked his hair, and as I did I saw tears fall from the corner of his eyes. He made no attempt to hide them.

"Harris it's just a dream," I said, holding him tighter than a mother with a child.

"There is no such thing as 'just a dream' Leah," he replied. "It's a message. It is trying to tell me something and I need to pay attention."

"What do you think it means?," I asked.

"The bear is a black cloud hanging over me and it will engulf my soul. I think it means we will only have a short time for happiness with each other on this earth. I don't think we will be together in this world."

I was finished with all of his esoteric thinking. I didn't know if his dad's Filipino blood was creeping into his psyche and there was truth behind it or if he was just losing his mind. Was it my fault because I kept saying I was afraid our love was too strong? But seriously, couldn't it have just been a stupid bad dream? Whatever it was, I started to think I had paid way too much attention to his reading material and I wanted no more of it.

I loved Harris more than I had known was possible, but for him to say this to me felt I had been stabbed straight through the heart. I wasn't sure if deep down he was having second thoughts about our future, or if it really was the dream that had brought on this fear. All forms of craziness trampled my mind. I looked over at his alarm clock and saw **1:44 AM**. I would need to leave soon and I didn't want to go with this hanging over us.

When I finally got some distance between my pain and his statement, I told him I didn't believe for a minute that was what the dream meant. I waited for him to reassure me, to affirm that I was making sense. But he didn't.

Instead he said, "I can't help it Leah, I think it is true."

Getting ready to go home I ached as if I'd already lost him. I couldn't place the sadness, but knew that the cruelest act of all would be for the universe to take him away from me. I didn't honestly know if I could handle that and come out the other end in one piece. In my deepest parts, I questioned whether Harris might be so in touch with another realm that he could look into it, or whether there was some type of mental instability that caused him to over think, over analyze and attach meanings to things that had none. I started to distrust the words, *intuition* and *collective unconsciousness*. They were just words, after all. Not everything had profound symbolic interpretations. I felt the very thing that had caused me to be so attracted to him was betraying me and making me wonder if he was alright.

All that night, the sky let loose. We were into monsoon season. We took the walk from his room to the front door of the dormitory together. It was the longest walk I had ever taken. In front of me lay nothing but questions with the answers I wanted for my life all behind the door of a dorm room decorated in blue.

Before I left him, we stood outside forever, soaked to the bone, clutching each other as if we would never meet again. In front of his barracks, the drainpipes purred with the sounds of water flowing. I could smell the rusty scent of wetness on old metal. The darkness of a moonless night in paradise had hidden us from prying eyes of men, but on that night, our kisses tasted of raindrops and tears mingled with the sea, and thus they told all the story of our passion.

Chapter 14

The rains that month came each day with determined spirit. In the mornings they pounded the earth and plummeted the grass into a fine creamed spinach. But in the afternoon the downpour was forgotten and rain was a mere mist. Harris recovered from his dream, thank God, and I was relieved it was no longer anything but an unpleasant memory. Harris confessed he loved rain more than sunshine. He said that PI rains were more insistent than the ones in Africa, but that he was fondest of the rains in Thailand. He said they always announced their comings and goings with claps of thunder so loud he could picture the Buddha striking a gong in heaven.

In Ohio, storms were threatening. The sky would blacken, the wind would blow and we would wait nervously for the siren warning us a tornado was in sight. I watched from his bedroom window while he worked on his poetry. We threw back the curtains and opened the glass to smell the freshness left on the lawn below. We made love with the lights off, dancing to the rhythm of the thunderous roars and flashes of light as they illuminated the night.

I decided that heaven must be a place where storms appear often.

In the middle of May, the winds started to change. It was still raining every day, but drops came down sideways pelting us from the east. Mike sat me down one evening to tell me he was going to take a temporary duty assignment to Guam. He said that he had volunteered for the assignment because he wanted to get away. It was the most honest conversation we had in the last twelve-and-a-half years.

I couldn't help but notice that his tone was different and he was much less cocky. I kept waiting for the bomb to drop, for him to tell me that he knew about Harris, but the conversation continued and ended without so much as a word to imply anything about my recent conduct.

I wasn't unhappy that he was leaving and he knew it.

"I know you don't care, I'm just letting you know it was my choice."

For the first time in a long while, I felt sorry for Mike. I wished he knew the strength of love

I had found.

During the next six weeks Lucy, Jess, Dana and I would have a home to ourselves.

When Harris heard the news, he was not as excited as I expected, but I think he was relieved knowing there would be six weeks without having to worry something would explode in our faces. Guam was a lot farther than Camp John Hay, so the thought of Mike turning up unannounced was most unlikely.

TDY for the guys meant extra money, so the ones that went usually lived it up while they were gone. Secretly, I was hoping Mike would go out a lot and find someone while he was there so our problem would be solved. The truth is, I had liked him in the early years. I even fancied I was in love when he asked me to marry him. Of course, back then, I had no way of knowing what it was really like to feel a true connection. Mike and I had no choice but to end up together.

Especially after Jessie was born. Poor Mike tried to do the right thing by offering to make us a family. Even though he waited until she was five years old do it. Before long, we both knew we shouldn't have married. But then I had Dana and Mike had joined the Air Force.

Harris and I had been together long enough to become careless in our displays. We no longer tried to hide our feelings in public. We went to a carnival together with the girls, which I knew was a bad idea even when I did it. All Mike would have had to do was ask Dana and the whole story would have come tumbling out of her mouth. He probably could have also gone to any officer's wife at the library, or the club, or the Mabuhay Café. You get the point. To his credit though, he said nothing and remained as he always had, emotionally detached.

Mike had no sooner packed his duffle bag when Harris arrived. I was so happy not to have to split time between him and the kids that at my suggestion, he quasi moved in with us. Obviously, I knew how wrong this was, but like everything else I was doing, I went ahead with it anyway. In those six weeks we ate together, played together and watched movies.

One evening after the kids had gone to bed, Lucy and I were in the kitchen having tea. With the help of Dana and Jessica her English had improved enough to where we could actually talk.

She dabbed her tea bag and dumped three generous spoons of sugar, and told me what was on her mind.

"I like him so much. He is better than other one."

I had been thinking that same thing. But "other one" was my husband and this man shouldn't be in his home.

The nights Harris stayed with us, I took the precaution of locking all the doors with a chain, including the one to my bedroom. I had the lock put on months ago, the kind that has a key, mostly because I didn't want Mike to come in and go through all of my stuff. I was pretty sure he didn't care enough to do that, but he could be a funny creature, not exactly predictable. Just when I thought he wouldn't care about something, he would go ballistic.

Harris slept beside me many nights during those weeks. Our bodies fit tightly together as we dozed off, in perfect sync, like the two halves of the heart necklace. I had never known such closeness. It was in the hours of sleep that my love for Harris grew stronger, and my resolve to keep our secret weakened. Like a good student, I had taken to heart what I heard Harris say as he quoted Rollo May; the animus and anima, the male to the female. He revealed through his poetry how he felt we had come to earth as twin flames, one soul in two bodies.

With the impending return of Mike, Harris was out. I no longer thought I could go on as I had before, knowing I had met my one true love and being forced to live apart. I wanted it all. I told Harris it was time to clear the air and come to honesty. He said the decision was mine as I was the one with the most to lose. And so, with firm determination I waited on the sofa for Mike as he unpacked his bags and doled out presents to the kids.

He tried to avoid a confrontation by saying he had planned to meet some of the guys after the flight, but I wouldn't let him go. It had taken so much effort for me to get to this place, I was afraid I might back down altogether if he put it off.

"Mike, you can't go right now. I really need to talk to you."

"Look," he sounded irritated, "whatever it is can wait, it's waited this long."

That should have been my clue.

"Mike please," I begged. "I have to talk to you, now."

With that, he slumped into a chair and looked me in the eyes.

"What do you need to tell me that I don't already know? Are you finally planning to tell me about *Sergeant* Harrison? Is that it? Because evidently you think I'm so stupid I don't know about him. You think I don't know he slept here while I was gone? You're an idiot if you thought for one second that I wouldn't find out."

I had been prepared to explain about love and soul mates and the rest of it, but I was caught off guard by this ambush.

"Let me tell you something," he continued.

"I have put up with more than any man should have to. You know me and I would have never done a thing like this to you. You and your little friend running all over the base with those enlisted men. Even up in Baguio. You thought I didn't know that too, didn't you?"

I guess I looked at him in disbelief, because then he said, "Don't you realize I work with Juan? God, Leah, how can you be so stupid?"

He was right.

"Mike, listen, it's not like you think."

He cut me off. "Oh no, it's exactly like I think. I know. You're in *love*."

The word, *love,* came out of his mouth like a swarm of bees fleeing a hive. My face dropped into my hands. I had no defense. It was true. I *was* stupid for thinking he didn't know and even more stupid for letting Harris stay in the house while he was TDY. I knew his friends. Those guys watch each other's backs. He probably had somebody watching me the whole time.

It was far too late to try to reason with him, to try to calm him down. He wouldn't let me get a syllable out. Each time I started to open my mouth, he got angrier. The veins on the side of his neck were standing up. I stood to back away. He had never hit me, but I was afraid that this time he might.

"I want you out. Do you hear me? And

soon. Find yourself another place to live or I am sending you back to the states."

In an act of self-preservation I bolted for the door. And just as fast he leaped in front of me. Reaching for the phone that sat on the coffee table, he yanked as hard as he could at the cord. The phone, the cord, peanuts, and a glass of mango juice shot across the room. When it landed, he grabbed the receiver and pressed it into my palm so hard I felt my bones bruise.

"Here," he added. "Call lover boy and tell him what I said."

Chapter 15

By the time I reached Rose's house, my hands had stopped shaking but there was still terror in my voice.

"Mike," was all I could manage. I left it to her to fill in the blanks.

"Shit, Leah." No offer of sorrow or empathy just 'shit.'

"I have to talk to Harris and he tore the phone cord out of the wall. There's a mess everywhere."

Doing a once over on my face she asked, "Did he hit you?"

I shook my head.

I almost wish he had. It would have served me right for what I had done. All I could say was, "It's such a mess. Everything is a mess."

As soon as Harris picked up the phone he knew.

"Look, you knew this would happen one day. We'll figure something out." Harris's calmness eased my mind. "This is just the beginning of our life together. He will let you go now and we can start the way we had planned all along."

He had a way of looking at what to me seemed catastrophic and turning it around into a positive. All the time I was wailing away about the unfairness of it all, Harris had decided to take action and make the situation work for us. His crazies the night of that dream were long gone and he was looking towards a new day.

"You are going to have to move out," he said.

I hadn't even gotten beyond the shock that now Mike knew about him.

"We'll need to find a place big enough for us and the girls and Lucy."

"Harris, I am still *married*. I can't just move in with you. What about the Air Force? I am a dependent wife, remember?"

"Later, you can go back to the states and get a divorce," he said casually, "but for now, you are going to have to get out of his house."

That afternoon, we took a walk through the tiny off base community of Plaridal I and we looked at three small houses. Each one was cuter than the one before. The only thing missing were the white picket fences. They were replaced by the typical concrete walls that all Philippine houses have off base. I wanted this change more than anything, but it didn't seem practical. I had no job. Harris was a staff sergeant who made next to no money. How did he think he could support us with his salary? I would have to get a job. But getting work on an air base wasn't easy, and by then, my reputation as an adulterous wife might even keep me from being hired.

Clark was incestuous by nature, but if you were a woman and you had the bad luck of being caught at the same thing the men did every day, that base could be a living hell.

I was angry with everybody, especially myself. From the outset, I guess it was certain. I had a limited about of time before the whole thing collapsed on me, but for some reason, maybe delusional, I imagined I would have more control over it. I hadn't thought far enough ahead. I was a victim of my own recklessness and hadn't anticipated the part after disclosure.

I was too consumed with my emotions to make plans. Now I was scurrying around trying to figure out how to move in myself and my kids with a man who was not my husband. This was all while I still had access to the commissary, the hospital, and every other base privileges because I was married to someone else. It was a twisted situation and it was getting more and more convoluted by the day.

Harris was either not worried or he was much better at handling stress. Part of me wanted him to get mad, too. But instead, he spent every spare moment of his day on a quest for a suitable house. He even offered to stay in the dorm while I moved, thinking that would help diffuse Mike's anger.

"He's going to want your base privileges if you move out."

He was right. There was no way Mike would allow me to live on Harris's money while using his name on base. Could I blame him? Like I said, twisted. At least I knew he would let the girls use the medical benefits.

The biggest problem with all this talk about moving was nothing fit Harris's price range. Those cute places with the palm trees in the front were twice the amount Harris could spend. Anything he could afford wasn't fit for a goat, much less a family of four. It was looking hopeless. And with Mike chanting, "Get out, and soon," I knew I had to figure something fast.

I wanted to go to Rose for help, just like I always did, but instead, the time I'd dreaded had come and the day I was going to say goodbye had arrived. In less than twenty-four hours she wouldn't be there when I needed her. Or even when I didn't. I took Padi Ko from my house to the base hotel. The movers had packed Rose up and the entire contents of her house were probably already on a boat somewhere between South Korea and Okinawa by now. She was just waiting for her flight.

Seeing Rose in the hotel room sent me down the rabbit hole. Again, I was in Alice's world where down was up and up was down. Everything was out of sync. I wanted more time. I wanted her to go back and live in her ancient barn with the very cool screened porch, on the cul de sac. I wanted her to drink the stupid Margaritas with me at the NCO club. And, I wanted to rewind time so that we could go to the Chicken Coop and have class at Wagner High. Time was not playing fair. I was not done with this part of my life and time was running out.

I stood in the doorway, almost afraid to enter. I looked around at her pile of luggage, her belongings strewn around the room. JJ was playing with the few toys she kept out for him. He flipped channels on the TV the way only a four-year-old could.

"Where is Lance?," I asked.

"He had to go and arrange for the transport of his bike."

I shook my head as if to say I understood, but what I wanted was for her to stop all this talk about leaving.

She was actually going to go through with it. I felt abandoned. I know I shouldn't have. Everyone has a right to have their chance at happiness and this was Rose's turn. But I had never been in the PI without her. I had never had a day when I had to wake up and face my thoughts alone. She was always around to give me advice or at least an ear. Sometimes, she was just giving me grief about my wardrobe. But, she was always there. Now all of a sudden she was going to be waking up somewhere else with a new friend to talk to and I had to understand it's just part of belonging to the government.

This is what military life is like. Here. There. Gone. Always moving and changing. Friends change, houses, schools, cars and furniture. You can collect masks or hats, or bar t-shirts that you pick up along the way, and they follow you from place to place, but you can't collect people because they are dispensable. We get orders, deploy, we get Short and we go back to the world. Yes, Rose was right, we were as military as our men. The ones we came here with and in Rose's case, the one she was leaving with.

"Rose, what am I going to do?"

"You mean about moving out?"

"I don't have any money. And you know Harris can't get a housing allowance. But I can't go back to the states."

"Loca, you know I'm not gonna lie to you. Yous got a mess on your hands. But you're the one who said when something is meant to be it's gonna happen. Right? Don't you think you and Harris are destined to be together?"

I knew I would never love another man as much as I did him, but, "I hope so," was my only reply.

"Soo, you'll have some tough shit to go through, but nothin' is ever as easy as we want it to be. She put her head down just enough so that I couldn't see the water welling up in her eyes.

I took a good long look at her. Wanting to memorize her face. I didn't want to close my eyes and not see the perfectly coifed hair and the expert make-up application. Those things that I secretly criticized her for doing and secretly admired at the same time.

There was no return date, no time to meet again. That bothered me. I sensed a shift in her, too. She was polished to perfection and ready to embark on her new life, so there should have been a glow, a spark, something to note a change was coming. When I move or travel to a new place, I am cleaned up more than any other time. I was sure Rose would be more glamorous than ever when she left. But I saw a small little thing, a blip, a something so tiny another person wouldn't have noticed. It nagged at me. Because between Rose and I there was a bond, tighter than just best friends. We were comrades in deception and sisters in spirit. I told myself to leave it alone, but something was amiss. I hoped she was making the right choice.

"Soo," she said, "I guess this is it huh?"

"Yeah, I guess it is." I couldn't think of anything else to say.

"Don't worry Loca, everything will work out alright." I wondered if she was referring to her or me.

"Everything is so messed up," I said.

"You know nothing stays the same." She grabbed me and hugged me tight. "Such is life."

She was smaller to me in that moment. Less dense, less vibrant. We talked that day for a long, long time. We shed thousands of tears and laughed at all the foolish fun we had together. Then, when it was finally time, when we could hold it back no longer, we had to say our goodbyes. I saw sadness in her eyes. She saw fear in mine.

"Soo," she said. "Keep it together Loca."

"Promise you'll write," I said. "Don't just say it and not do it."

"Shit you know me. Yous really think I'm gonna sit down and write a letter?"

I laughed hard through my sniffles. I knew she was telling the truth. She wouldn't write, not even one stinking word.

"Then we'll call," I said. "It's expensive, but at least once a month. Okay?"

"Deal," she said as she kissed me on both cheeks. "Besides Kadena isn't that far. You can visit. Anyhows, if I don't see yous there, someday we'll end up in the real world again. And it's for sure I'll see you on the other side."

Then in typical Rose fashion, she said, "Sooo, get the hell outta here before yous flood the damn place."

And that was it. The door closed. She was gone.

Chapter 16

Before Rose's plane landed in San Juan, I answered the phone to an unexpected caller.

"Mrs. Leah Holden?" I didn't recognize the voice.

"Yes it is," I said.

"Good morning Mrs. Holden, this is Colonel Brakeman from the 31st Airborne Division. I am you husband's commander. I need to see you in my office this afternoon at 1400 hours.

It was more a direct order than an invitation. No other way to answer except to say that I would be there. And nothing to think other than this couldn't be good.

I arrived at 1352 just to make sure I didn't do anything to offend the commander. I had assumed that the great colonel would have an office the size of a small palace, but instead, he was located in one of the portables right near the Base Education office.

As I walked up the steps to the 31st Airborne Headquarters, I glanced over at the Base Education trailer. That was where Rose and I had gone that chilly day in January to sign up for Business English and Anatomy 101. Since then, I had taken Physiology 101, Psychology 101 and Comparative Religions. All with Harris by my side.

The inside of the headquarters office was no plusher than the outside. Metal chairs lined the sides of the walls, if you could call them that. Mostly, the walls were made out of aluminum and painted an off white to make you think they were real walls. The requisite recruitment posters and certificates of accomplishment decorated the waiting area outside the CO's office. I figured the décor meant it was not good to get too relaxed about why you have been summoned, but I had a horrible hunch. Put it this way, I had never been called, addressed by name, or asked to visit a CO in the entire time Mike had been in the military. I was sure this meant the colonel had me in the sights of his rifle and the firing squad had been readied.

"You may go in now," said the young airman who sat sentry over the CO's front door. He was only a child, but looked to be most impressed with how important a job he had managed to wrangle out of the USAF. The office, itself, was no more lavish than the waiting area. Except for the colonel's desk. I had a feeling he probably had invested in the desk himself, as it was made of what looked like an exceptionally expensive piece of teakwood. If the idea was to look masculine and imposing, it did the job nicely. The top of the desk had nothing at all on it other than a notebook placed directly in front of him, and the nameplate carved out of wood that was decorated with caribou and other scenes from the PI-like palm trees and coconuts. Everyone in the military had one of those nameplates. They were dirt-cheap at the shops on Perimeter Road and even if an airman didn't have a desk to put it on, you could be sure he invested in one for the future. Good thing it was there too, because I had forgotten the good officer's name in my nervousness and there was nothing like a nice wood plaque as a reminder.

The colonel's grey hair was buzzed to a perfect military cut, clean around the ears and off the neck. He looked down at me through his glasses and read from the note pad. Then he scribbled a few lines, took off the glasses and addressed me, directly.

"Have a seat, Mrs. Holden." He motioned to the only available chair. Another one made of hard metal. "I had a talk with your husband earlier and I have learned some very distressing facts about your behavior since you arrived on base."

I braced myself.

"He discussed the fact that you have been seeing an enlisted man," he said, looking down at the paper, again. "A Staff Sergeant Harrison from 330th?" I thought he wanted an answer but he continued on.

"I am not going to tell you how to run your personal affairs, Mrs. Holden, but I am here to protect the interests of my staff. Your husband has done an outstanding job of distinguishing himself as an officer in the Air Force and I don't have to tell you that this type of marital problem can severely affect his morale. "

"No, sir," I mumbled.

"The reason you are here is because we are going to come to some understanding and it is going to be today. I will not have the morale of Capt. Holden jeopardized by this extramarital affair that you are involved in. You are here at the goodwill of the United States Air Force. That requires you to conform to certain standards. It also means your status can change at any moment if I feel you are a detriment to my troops. Do you understand what I am saying to you?"

"I think so," I answered. I tried to hold my knees as still as possible to keep them from trembling.

"Well, just so that we are clear, let me spell it out. You are in the not so enviable position today where you are going to be forced to make a choice. This choice will not be made tomorrow. Nor will it be made sometime in the future. You need to make that choice now. You have just one of two options, as I see it. Number one: If you wish to divorce your husband, orders will be typed up right now and you will be off the base and on a plane back stateside within 48 hours. That is a very reasonable decision at this point. However, with the charge of adultery against you, and mind you, that would be the charge, the military will grant temporary custody of the children to Capt. Holden and you will return to the states, alone. Number two: And, this, mind you, is only an option because you husband has been gracious enough to allow it. You may continue to stay on in base housing, with your husband, if you are committed to working through your problems and repairing the damage that has been done to your marriage. That means mandatory marriage counseling as well. Personally, after what I heard from him, I want you to know I advised him against it; but I will honor his wishes and it is his wish to take you back. In that case, of course, you do understand, quite clearly that under no circumstances will you be allowed to associate with Sergeant Harrison again. That means as of this moment. You are to break off all connections with the Staff Sergeant and if I should ever hear of you being in his company, even in the most innocent of circumstances, the retribution in this case will not only be yours. As a member of the military, Sergeant Harrison is under the UCMJ order not to fraternize with the wife of another military member. He has broken that code and can be court martialed. Any further indiscretion and I promise you, I will see to it myself that is exactly what happens. He will likely be stripped of what rank he does have, possibly sent to the brig or dishonorably discharged. In other words, Mrs. Holden, this man's military career is on the line here. Now, if you have the feelings that your husband says you claim to have for Sergeant Harrison, you are going to think long and hard about what I am saying to you. I am going to keep him out of it for now, and as long as you do what you need to do, he won't be involved. Now, do we understand each other?"

"Yes, sir," I said. "I understand."

He didn't need to ask me if I had made a decision. I walked away and collapsed on the front step of the portable. If this was a war, I had been defeated. All that was left to do was find a white sheet.

Mike didn't return home that night. Thank

God. I couldn't have stood to look at him or hear his horrendous music blaring. I shut my bedroom door, locked the chain so he couldn't get in, and sat on the bed rocking myself. I could imagine myself locked inside a mental hospital, thrown in a padded cell. I tried to call Harris several times, but I wasn't sure of the conversation we would have. A conversation about what?

The hours went by and no Harris. Not at the dorm, not at his duty station. I was sure that Colonel Brakeman had reneged on his promise and gotten to him first. That had to be it. He was refusing to answer my calls.

I couldn't cry. I shook too much to hold the phone steady any longer. In one week, Rose was gone, Harris was missing in action, and life as I knew it was over. I was stuck with making a "decision" when I knew no decision I made could ever be right.

I threw the blankets over my head and tried to hide from my pain. I lay like that for hours and then finally, near midnight, the back door bell rang. Without even trying to fix my disheveled hair and face, I went to the door thinking Mike had forgotten his key. Harris stood in front of me. I looked beyond him. He was alone, and his bicycle was leaning against that old water pump.

"His car isn't outside. Is he here?" he asked,

hesitating before coming in.

"No," I said.

"I was afraid to just rush over, but I had to tell you." He wrapped his arms around me and kissed me. He finally noticed the worried look. "Hey, hey it's okay. Don't."

He smoothed my hair as he had done dozens of times before. He had no idea what was wrong.

He smiled broadly.

"I found a place. It's a bit of a drive, but the jeepney will take us to the main road and then we can get a trike to the house. I told the guy to hold it until tomorrow. I'm sure you'll love it."

"And," he added, holding me closer, "you're not going to believe the price. It's less than 100USD a month."

Then he backed up and looked me in the eye. "See I told you we could work things out."

"No Harris," I said. My voice was dry and cold. He watched me curiously.

"What do you mean, *No*?"

"I mean 'no,' I can't move in with you."

"Yeah, I know. You and the girls will stay there. I'll come when I'm off duty. I'll be there unofficially."

"Harris, you don't understand. I can't move. I mean…I'm not moving. I am going to stay with Mike."

Harris stood still for what was probably a

little less than a minute and felt like more than an hour. He stared at me and squinted his eyes in disbelief.

"Say that, again."

"I said I am going back to my husband."

He half chuckled. "You don't mean that."

I could no longer look him in the eye. I was focusing on his name. With my eyes I traced the blue stitching that spelled *Harrison* just above his heart, and when he spoke to me, it was his lips I looked at, instead.

"I mean it, Harris."

"Oh, my God," he said. He literally spun around in place. "I don't believe you. You don't even love him. You never did. What the hell are you doing?"

I wanted to go to him and hold him close, and tell him it wasn't true. That I would never do this to him. That I would never hurt him this way, but instead, I backed away and just said, "I'm sorry."

"Leah, please. Don't do this. Tell me what happened. What has he done to you? I'll kill him," he said. "Did he threaten you?"

"No," I lied. "It's just better this way."

We were faced off, standing right in the middle of the kitchen, and in an attempt to change my mind, he moved in and kissed me longer and more passionately than I think he ever had before.

"Now you tell me you don't feel that. Because I don't believe you, not for one minute. The only way I will believe you is if you can look at me and say you don't love me."

God help me, I thought. *Help me get through this.*

Without batting an eye, I lifted my head, stared straight at him and answered, "I'm going back to Mike."

"Say it." he yelled. "Go ahead, if you can say it, I will go and never come back. Go ahead, go ahead." He insisted. "Say you don't love me."

And then as he stood with his hand on the kitchen door, one foot in my world and one out, I held my breath and begged him silently for forgiveness for what I was about to do. Then I uttered the words I thought would never come out of my mouth, and as he backed out of the door, I said, "I don't love you."

Harris shook his head from side to side and screamed. "*No.*" Not once, but over and over and over again. He jumped over the two stairs that led from the back porch and he was still saying it when he picked up the bike and rode away. He didn't look behind. I had to hold myself. I wanted to follow him. To fix it and tell him I lied, and that I am such a damn good liar that he believed me, and that I really loved him more than I had ever loved anyone, and I couldn't live without him.

But I knew better, so I only followed him as far as that stupid old pump, and as I pressed my legs against it for support, I heard his voice. He moaned like a wounded animal bellowing at the moon. It was from the depths of his soul and it made me cringe, I could feel the hurt in my bones. I had never heard the sound of a man dying, but I thought I recognized it as that. As I watched him round the corner and turn onto the highway, I prayed for him to stop, but instead he cried louder, *"Nooooooooooooooooooooooooooooooooooooooooo."*

The side of the pump couldn't hold me. I dropped to the ground and wept. While I waited for his howling to fade, a searing sting ran through my head and down my spine. And that's when I knew I had been cut in half. My pleading to the universe, "God please help him," did no good because the farther away he rode, the louder I thought I heard the screams and the more awful it sounded. I listened to his sobs and his voice echoing the word, *"No,"* long into the night.

Sitting on the warm cement, I was paralyzed until it was over. I felt it was the last night of love in my life and so I stayed weeping by the water pump until I was left with nothing but a long, lonely silence.

Chapter 17

I went to bed that night and didn't get up. The gaping hole in my heart burned so deep that I had no strength to stand. I wanted to undo the pain I had inflicted, but I knew it had become part of the story and could not be undone. Like committing murder.

Consolation was impossible. My mate, my twin flame, one who held the other half of my heart, was gone. I retreated once again to the place that gave me solace. Or at least a silent space to grieve alone. I loved Harris more than I ever thought possible, but I forced us to be apart. I told myself he must never know why, lest he do some wrong for which he would pay an even bigger price that the one he was already paying. I feared for his safety. When I heard his cries that night, they etched a permanent scar on my soul. I heard them again each time I drifted near sleep. I might as well have run over him with a car. I knew I wanted it done to me.

I told Harris it was too strong. I knew the danger in that. I foretold our demise. And I remembered his dream. He feared it, too. Star-crossed lovers always die in the end. Unfortunately, this time I was one of the lovers and my life hung in the balance.

Nobody and nothing made a difference. Not my children, not my future, not anything, nor anyone. There was only pain. And that pain meant I locked myself away for over a month and cried. Every day. All day. Until I lost track of reality. There were never enough tears. I didn't know how to stop them.

Jessie told me she and Dana came to my room each day to see what was wrong with me, but I sent them away to be with Lucy. She said Mike sometimes found me sitting on the back step in the middle of the night, and he or Lucy would tell me it was late and time to come in. I lost over fifteen pounds that month and looked like a stick. But none of this do I remember.

One day, I recall thinking that I had to end the pain and pay for my sins. I doubted that Harris realized the sacrifice was made for him, too. Confusion set in. First I said I couldn't tell him and then I begged to have the chance. I wanted to know what was happening to him. Was he okay? Did he miss me? Did he cry anymore? Or was it only me that was doing the crying for both of us?

I decided that I either had to live with the consequences or die as a result. I sat on the bed with the same dirty clothes I had worn for I guess, that entire month. I saw a bottle of the sleep medicine I used to shut out the world and keep obsessive thoughts from running rampant in my brain. I thought it would be better to take them all at once and sleep forever than to stay behind and live without Harris. I took one, two, three, four little pink and white capsules, and then I stopped. What would happen if I did die? Who would take care of Jessica and Dana? Their dad? He would be the role model that would teach my children what love was in this world.

I once told Harris that the two people I loved most in the world were my children and that they would always come first. I had to mean it. Even if the man I loved more than I loved myself was gone. Any pain I had needed to be second to their having a mother.

I woke up two days later, so my decision to live was made for the same reason I thought I wanted to die. Love kills and gives life all in the same being.

Though losing Harris still tore through every cell of my body, I had to get on with life. My daily routine slowly went back to normal on the outside, but in my head the thoughts were always the same. I wanted him back. I wanted to know if he was hurting as much as I was. I wanted to see his face, just once. No, that's a lie. I wanted to see his face forever.

I started to go places and take small steps at becoming myself, again. Mike and I went to couples counseling. And though I lied in front of Mike to keep up the charade, when alone with the counselor, I never pulled punches. I told him I would not stay with Mike in the end no matter what anyone did to try to fix the marriage. But I went because that is what the USAF said I had to do to keep my family intact until I could get the hell out.

Our meetings were at the base hospital on Wednesday afternoons at 1600 and I usually went alone. I would meet Mike and we would often leave together. Such a lovely couple we made. But Wednesday nights at home were not enjoyable. They were tense and sometimes on those evenings I even vomited. Mike went into the sessions with his typical air of superiority and I was, of course, the one who had done the damage. I couldn't defend myself because I knew it was my weakness that caused the problem. I felt too much and I wanted love, freedom and the pursuit of happiness.

One Wednesday, I arrived at the hospital early. The weather was so humid I needed a shower 15 minutes after stepping outside. On days like that I always went early so I could cool off and look less sweaty for my appointment. The taxi dropped me off in front of the building as it always did. As I walked through the double doors, there he was. Standing by the flight surgeon's office. He looked well. I looked thin. He was in his green military fatigues with his name written in blue, just above his heart. We saw each other at the same moment. He met my eyes with his but gave no expression and then he looked away. My heart dropped and I could feel my insides roll. I was sick. I wanted to stop him, to say something, but I remembered the admonition of Colonel Brakeman. I couldn't chance any conversation. From the look on Harris's face, he wasn't about to give me the opportunity.

I knew right then how deeply he, too, had been wounded. I asked him silently for forgiveness so many times as I lay in bed and hid myself away from the world, but when face-to-face with the man I had been so close to, I had no words. He had none, either. We didn't part because we grew tired of each other. We ended because of timing, of circumstance. The synchronicity of events that conspired to bring us together in the first place had now done the same thing in reverse. Whose fault was that? Was it really Mike who did it? Or should I lay this at the feet of Colonel Brakeman? Was it the

Uniformed Code of Military Justice? Did the blame belong to me, or to Harris, because we acted on a love that we knew we had no right to feel? Or was this simply the fault of God?

In another place and time, we might have had the happily ever after that I imagined for us. But in another place and time, we may never have met at all. We may have crossed in the night, as they say, never knowing the other existed. So I went home with my husband. I ate dinner with my children. I read a story to Dana, talked to Jessie about gymnastics lessons. I asked Lucy to do a load of wash before morning, and then I shut the door to my bedroom and cried another thousand tears. There were still so many more that could have come.

Chapter 18

When the phone rings at 4:27 AM and you live half a world away from family, the most dreadful thoughts cross your mind. The ring of a telephone in the middle of the night always felt ominous. I don't know why it never seemed to be true of daytime calls, but when awakened from a sound sleep, the imagination always goes straight towards tragedy.

"Hey Loca."

"Rose, where are you?" I was happy to hear her voice.

"I'm in Okinawa. Lance and I are married."

"Wow. Congratulations." I said, happy for her, and at the same time sad for myself.

"We got here yesterday. Sooo how's life with you and Harris?"

Finally, I was able to tell her the whole sordid story.

"God, Leah I can't believe it. Soo, you're back with Mike?"

"I live with him, yes, and no, I can't see Harris anymore, but you know as well as I do, I will never be back with Mike."

We talked much longer than we should have, but she didn't rush me off the line and she gave me time to say all the things that I had wanted to tell her for the past three months. Then I noticed she was sounding tired.

"Hey Rose maybe we'd better hang up so you can get some rest. I'll bet you have jet lag huh?"

She didn't answer.

"Are you doing alright?," I asked. "You know, with the diabetes and everything?"

I hadn't given much thought to Rose's condition since that day I found her with the insulin. She functioned so normally that it was easy to forget that she really did have a problem. But she was still grossly unconcerned about how she plied herself with booze and sweets, and I figured that couldn't be a good thing.

Still, she didn't answer.

"Are you okay?" I asked, hoping she would give me some idea of what was wrong.

"Sure, I'm fine, just messed up a dose of insulin that's all."

Something didn't ring true.

"Are you sure that's all it is Rose, because you don't usually do that. But I guess with the move and all, it's...."

"Loca, that's not it."

"Rose, what's wrong?"

"While I was at home, I was in the hospital for a little while. I got back some tests. One was to measure my kidney function."

I realized what was coming could not be good. I braced myself.

"The doctor told me that I'll probably need dialysis in a year, or maybe two at the most."

Then she hesitated.

"I thought I had more time."

I couldn't believe my ears. She had known that this was happening and she had said nothing.

"What do you mean, you 'thought you had more time'? How long have you known this was a possibility?"

"It's always a possibility with diabetes, Leah," she said.

I knew that, but I was asking: Why did she say she thought there was time? It implied prior knowledge. She had never said she was in serious danger of kidney failure.

"Okay, so you've known the *probability* for how long?"

"Awhile."

"*Awhile*?"

"About five years, I guess."

I expected her to say about a week.

"What are they going to do about it?" I asked.

"Nothing to do." She sighed.

I was sure that the doctors had warned her about her diet and lifestyle, but I knew Rose. She wasn't much for taking advice.

But I attempted to give it a try. "Don't you think you should watch it a little more? You know, be more careful about your diet and…."

"Leah, what don't you get? IT'S TOO LATE." She yelled at me.

Her voice cracked. "I'm gonna do what I want for as long as I can, cause life doesn't give you guarantees."

I felt bad. I had been jealous. She and Lance were married and Harris and I had parted. Her happily ever after was not necessarily so happy after all.

It was far past dawn when I finally got down to rest again. With Rose in Okinawa married to Lance, they had come full circle. She was beginning a new part of her life and at the same time another part of it was ending. Dialysis was not a death sentence anymore, it was a waiting game, but it was not a way to live with any quality, certainly not for a person like Rose. I couldn't imagine her hooked up to the machines and spending days sitting in the hospital waiting while her body filtered out the waste that should have been done by her failed kidneys. It wasn't a picture I wanted to see. She said her sister might be willing to donate. So that was hopeful. Yes, that was excellent because a solution just had to be out there.

When I was a child, I always used to complain when I thought something 'wasn't fair.' My sixth grade teacher, Mr. Brown, would just give me a kindly but stern look, and say, "Leah, don't get in the habit of thinking life should be fair because it isn't."

I wanted to find him and make him take it back.

Before sleeping, I floated back to the days when Rose acted as if she didn't have a care in the world. We were doing the best we could to live life in this place that we called our home, even though it was thousands of miles from where we came. Rose and I, Lance and Harris, we were a team. Now we were a memory. In the end, I guess all of us just become memories. It was a sobering thought and the melancholy of life's impermanence visited me as I drifted off to sleep.

Yes, Rose, you are right. The truth is, life doesn't give us any guarantees.

Chapter 19

As the time neared for Harris to leave, I knew I'd have to step up my attempts to see him. I tried to be everywhere all at once, in hopes that we could catch glimpses of each other. Even still, I didn't have much faith that he would want to see me. The meeting at the hospital that Wednesday was a sign, and it told me he probably would rather I stay away. I just knew if I told him why I did what I did, then the anger he was having, or the pain, or the grief, whichever it was, would be lifted. I realized, as the days grew close for his departure, the best time to reveal why I went back to Mike would be as he was boarding the plane. Then there would be no chance of any tryst that could get him thrown in the brig, or a scene with Mike that could do the same. I had decided to go to the air terminal on the day he was supposed to fly out. I would then make a last ditch attempt to explain my actions.

I called Rose the day before he was leaving. I was getting scared and I considered backing out of the plan.

"No, you have to do it Loca."

She had told me many times that although my motive for not telling him was noble, it wasn't smart. Not exactly the way she put it, but the gist was the same.

"You're a fuckin' idiot. You shoulda said somethin' to him when yous had the chance."

'Fucking idiot' or not, I did what I thought was right at the time and now I was really afraid he would either ignore me and just give me the brush-off when we met.

I tried to time my arrival at the base terminal so that he would be finished with out-processing. I knew the schedule well. I checked to find out when the Flying Tigers left for California. They departed 1600 each day. So, three days prior to his out-processing date, I went over to the airport and waited to see how long it took for the entire group to finish paperwork and customs. After they completed the formalities, they waited for at least an hour before it was time to board the plane. Most of them went to the lunch truck outside the building and came back with sandwiches. Or they simply sat and talked to each other. It was at that point that I wanted to catch Harris. It would be a wonderful farewell. I had dreamt of it so many times I had the details worked out perfectly.

On August 6th, I spent over an hour getting ready. I abandoned my jeans for a dress. With my newly thinner-than-ever body, everything I wore looked good. I made up my face with just enough makeup to look naturally pretty and I curled my hair.

I paced the floor of the living room while I waited for the taxi to arrive. I had to sit several times because even with the Air Con blaring, the heat was so intense in summer that my hair and makeup would have been ruined had I continued to move around. The taxi was late.

"When is my taxi arriving? I need to be at the airport at 1030." I called in a panic.

I didn't deny it when the dispatcher got the impression my insistence on promptness was because I was taking a flight myself.

"Well hurry up." I shouted at him.

As I rode in the backseat, I was hypnotized by the jacaranda trees that lined the highway and I started playing my version of how things would go once I reached the airport.

I would see Harris across the room, just as he picks up his duffle to walk through the double doors. I would yell to him to stop. He would turn and drop his bag. We would meet in an embrace of kisses and tears. I would disclose my real reason for parting with him.

Then after declaring our everlasting love, I would say I was going back to get a divorce. He would say he'd wait. The sergeant at arms would call for him to hurry up and we would share one more kiss, one that needed to last. With my hands pressed against the window, my eyes would follow him down the tarmac and up the stairs of the plane. Before he disappeared, he would do that little turn, throw his hand in the air, and mouth the words, "I love you."

Too many movies.

Everybody was shipping out. MPs were barking orders. An ocean of uniforms so thick that faces were lost, and only the dress blues and green duffle bags stood out. There was no way I was going to be able to pick Harris out of a crowd like this. Being five-two didn't help, having to look up to see heads. No room to maneuver, no room even to breathe.

I headed for the NCO lounge thinking he may have gone there to get away from the crowded room. He hated crowds. Then I wandered around and thought of paging him, but the loudspeaker was on the other end of the terminal, and the idea of getting across the mob with boxes being slammed and bags being thrown seemed insurmountable. I had no chance of making it all the way in one piece.

More than an hour later, after being pushed,

squeezed, and having my toes smashed twice, I saw a man who looked like Harris standing in a corner by the Stars and Stripes rack. As I moved closer to the rack, I realized I was mistaken.

I walked over to the window, the same one in my fantasy. I gazed out at the tarmac from the spot where I was supposed to be when he turned to wave goodbye.

The plane boarded from both ends, two lines and two staircases, and even though I watched one first and then the other, from I where I stood I wouldn't have made out my own mother in the fray.

I saw the plane take off knowing that the man I loved was on it. I had no pictures of him. No phone number, no way to tell him I had made a big mistake.

I had ruined my last opportunity. He was now on his way to the USA and I was in the PI for another two years.

I had lost him all over again. I went back to bed, back to crying, back to Mike.

Chapter 20

The new base commissary opened a couple of weeks later. I made it a point to go at least once a week since it was upgraded and they actually had things in stock. Our first Thanksgiving in the Philippines was a nightmare. The kids and I had gone to buy ingredients for our veggie dinner. Cranberries for sauce, pumpkin, pie shells, spices, sweet potatoes. The usual. But somebody had beaten us to the punch. Or should I say a bunch of somebodies. I felt like Old Mother Hubbard. No sugar, no pumpkin, cranberries, or any other item that was needed to pull together a real Thanksgiving dinner. I secretly rejoiced when I saw that there weren't any turkeys left either. We ended up having potato salad, coleslaw, and baked beans. I told Jessica and Dana that is what Thanksgiving in the Philippines was supposed to be like. Besides, we ate outside to make it like a big picnic. You couldn't do that for Thanksgiving in Ohio.

One day, while pushing the cart down the cereal aisle, I felt a tap on the shoulder. It was Denise.

"Long time, no see." She grinned.

We couldn't really call each other friends, but we got along well enough. Even though Harris and I visited Denise and Alex from time to time, I never felt close to them. So it was inevitable that once Harris and I broke up, my friendship with them had no foundation. I suspected that she hadn't talked to me on purpose and I wasn't surprised that our contact now was only accidental.

"Yeah, another commissary trip," I said, staring at the Cheerios display. I hadn't realized it until I saw her, but even talking with her was painful. Too many raw memories. I wished I hadn't run into her.

"You must not be eating much of that food." She looked down at the packages in my cart. "You've lost weight."

It looked like more than it was, but on a small person, even the twelve pounds that managed to stay off after hell month seemed huge.

She tried her best to keep it light. I could sense her discomfort.

"And how are your girls?" She tapped Dana on the head. "Wow, you know it's weird running into you again. Alex wanted to invite you over but…."

I stopped her in mid-sentence. "Did you talk to Harris before he left?"

The truth was the only thing we had in common was Harris, and now she was my only link to him.

"Yeah. He was at the house last Thursday. We had a goodbye dinner for him."

"I thought he was leaving on the 6th?" I asked.

"Yeah, he was supposed to, but they held a bunch of guys over for the war games."

So that was it. The whole time I was at the airport waiting to see him off he wasn't even there. He had no idea that I was trying to reach him and now I had no way to do it. Once again, fate had intervened and had done one hell of a job keeping us apart. I had been grieving because he was gone and he was still here. Now that I understood he was really gone, the process began all over again. I felt like I would never fully recover because I was never going to stop thinking about him.

After the girls went to bed, I sat on the top step of the back porch with time alone and a tall glass of Calamansi juice. The night breeze, though still hot, was less humid, so I pulled the rubber band that held my mass of curls, to let the wind lift them. This porch was a lonely place, the scene of a crime. It was the one place on Earth that witnessed my treason. The old water pump knew my misery. I sat with my arms folded and soothed myself with music. Angela Bofill had just released a new song, *Time to Say Goodbye*. I played it until the tape was smooth and the lyrics lost their power over me. But I wasn't only remembering. I needed a plan.

I still had so much time left on Clark. With no more Harris and no Rose, more than anything, I wanted to leave. No money forces you to do things you never thought yourself capable of. I used to walk down the road and think about the teenage prostitutes along Friendship Highway. Most of them were no older than sixteen. No child grows up thinking, "When I get older, I will move to a bar, live in a stinky sex-filled back room with twelve other girls, and for five dollars, I will go with any man who will have me." And for those five dollars if they were lucky, they got a bed in a military dorm for the evening. It's all about the money. Parents sold their daughters. From the five dollars, the girl got two, the bar got three, and most of what she made went back home to feed her mother, father, brothers, and sisters (if they were still too young to be 'bar girls').

I was no better. Pretending that inside that back door was a marriage. Living with a man for money. Sometimes, now I look at talk shows. I see the women black and blue, beaten down with fists and words and I brace myself, waiting for the stupid idiot in the audience who asks, "Why didn't you just leave him?"

Ask me. I know why. No damn money.

With enough money, I would have walked away from Mike so fast a train would have derailed trying to keep up the pace.

I had no reason to be there. Just to soak up the tropical breeze and sit idle for the next couple years of my life? Wait for the next installment of Mike and Leah: The never-ending saga of pain and desperation? If I didn't start making plans soon, I would be on my way to the next location, penniless, jobless and stuck. Unfortunately, moneymaking opportunities didn't abound for dependent wives. The hierarchy was designed to keep us 'dependent.' Locals got first choice and then as a last resort, we would be called. But, even that wasn't easy. Too many wives, too few jobs.

The waiting list was endless. I had put my name on it shortly after I arrived that first month. Over two years had passed and still no call. Obviously, I had to come up with a better plan.

Even as I sat in the night, catching the cool air, and mulling over the options, I knew there weren't a lot of options to mull. The favored career of women in the PI didn't suit me, and thanks to cheap maid service, babysitters weren't needed. I considered exporting things from the Philippines. A good business, for sure. Many lovely trinkets were stamped, "Made in the Philippines," but a business like that required two things and I had neither: startup cash to purchase and mail, and someone trustworthy on the other end to sell.

Last option: Not too legal, but not so immoral. At least that is how I rationalized it.

Chapter 21

The bus from Marshall Highway took me all the way to the main gate. On the way out, you were supposed to stop and show the guards what you were taking off base. I never had anything to show, so I was never stopped.

I walked through the steel bars like I was being released from jail. Inside the base, it was all orderly and contained. Outside, the sensory carnival was as thick as the inside was sterile.

A little shirtless man jumped in front of me saying something about, "Tricycle. Where you want to go?"

I was used to the stench at the gate by now. The mixture of urine and barbeque was hardly noticeable to me anymore, but when I did recognize the scent, I had to wonder if the men who peed on the side of the base wall were simply reliving themselves or making a political statement.

The bright colors of jeepneys and trikes, and

teeny, tiny ladies. They wore stretch jeans that grabbed their little no-ass bottoms. They balanced three-inch heels that wobbled in the stones and potholes and probably did a lot of damage if some unseemly guy tried to short change them. Barbequed everything for sale, newspapers blowing the smoke to tempt you, empty San Miguel's lined the walkway in no particular order, and me.

In the midst of all the noise and confusion, I walked with purpose. No need for money changers or transport, I was an old timer. I knew exactly where I was going. I wiped the sweat from my brow and tucked my bangs, which I was now rethinking, back into the ponytail. My t-shirt stuck to my sides. I was musty and dirty. I kept walking.

I was thousands of miles away from my good Catholic upbringing, in an even more Catholic country. I was turning the corner, headed down the alley towards pushers and prostitutes and all that was seedy and ugly. The under belly of what this place was all about. God, I was happy I had come here.

Baby's barbeque stand was around the next corner. I remember when Rose and I walked the same streets. I had passed the first test. No formal introduction, no work. Baby never forgot a face. She had to be sure-eyed in her business. She needed to know who was watching her.

Harris and I used to walk this neighborhood, too. Only, we did it at night just to see how it lit up. How the energy spilled into the street. Hand in hand we passed by bars and discos. Sometimes, we would pop in to see the topless girls on the stage. Heels and string bikinis. I had to keep close hold of Harris on Fields Avenue. Eager bar girls would try to steal him right out of my arms. Once, a dancer saw me walk in with Harris and she hopped straight off the stage. She cuddled up to him, turned her backside in the air and sensuously rubbed her hands up and down her ass. Another shoved her boobs in his face and squeezed her own nipples, mouth open mimicking ecstasy. All the while gyrating to a song by Foreigner. I guess it was funny at the time, but I knew what these girls were selling was the source of many a marriage gone wrong.

Sometimes, we ventured into Baby's territory. We would wave or stop for just a quick chat. Rose said to keep her as a friend. So I did. We sat on the tree stumps in front of her stand to rest. Those were nights when her transactions were slow and Harris and I were in no hurry, with no particular destination. She never talked about her business. She never asked me if I was interested. I never asked her what she did.

She was sitting on that same old rattan stool when I walked up to her barbeque stand. Counting money under the table. Baby—I didn't know if it was her real name, but it fit the round face and pudgy body. She had permed her hair since I last saw her and now it looked like spiral black ribbons framing her face.

Maybe it was in my eyes. I've been told by many people that I can't hide my emotions, but she dispensed with the pleasantries. She knew what I wanted.

"You want work?"

I was startled.

"Yes," I answered.

"You want work today?" Her name belied the directness in her voice. This was business.

"Yeah, I guess." It looked like ready or not, I was going to work.

"Okay. You come." So I followed her. Through another alley, to a doorway covered by pink plastic beads, and into a dark cement hallway. She stopped at the end, took a ring of keys from her pocket, found the right one, and showed me in.

Just an open bulb hanging from the ceiling lit the room. Attached only on a wire held by a hook. Cinderblocks and cement. Gray on gray. A pyramid of tan boxes occupied the center.

"Today client come five thirty. Base lady tell

me she is coming to bring shopping, but she not come. You work good. Get good commission."

Looked as if I had arrived at the right time.

"Need many things. You got cigarettes left on ration?"

"Sure," I said.

Since I didn't smoke, I never used my CEX ration card for cigarettes. People told me that was stupid. Most said I should buy some and sell them on base. Even for a dollar or two more. I had never seen the point. But now I saw it. What would it look like if all of a sudden I started buying my entire allotment when I never even bought one carton before that? I started to get scared.

"How many you can get me?"

I thought five would be good. That was half the amount allowed. Not too suspicious.

"Marlboro red, hard pack. Okay?" She pointed to some stacks at the other side of the room. "Need Spam. You get six. And some red apples, one dozen."

The list went on. Carnation powdered milk. Snickers candy bars. Reese's Cups. Oranges and JB Scotch.

Baby even fronted me the money. The problem was I had to get it all off base. I couldn't take the bus. Even though I knew most of the time an innocent looking American could get away with a lot. MPs aren't usually going to be bothered about what you are carrying on or off base, but this was a big load. And I wasn't about to be busted with a bag full of rationed goods. I took Padi Ko, instead.

Just to be sure, I folded a few old clothes on top of the stuff I was delivering. If I was stopped they would see a nice housewife taking used baby clothes to the poor. I thought it was brilliant. Espionage. Covert operations and all that.

When we reached the checkpoint, the guards barely turned to see who was there. I had always heard the only reason they turned to look at all was to see if an officer was passing by. That required a salute. Forgetting to salute an officer, in their minds, was far worse than letting some civilian off base with commissary goods.

Not trusting anyone, especially the drivers from Padi Ko, I made the old man let me off in the Balibago subdivision where I got a tricycle. It's hard to describe a tricycle. It was sort of like a motorcycle with a sidecar, only flashier and with a hint of the decoration that one usually only sees on jeepneys. That's where I found Javier. He had those bumps that teenagers get, so his face was a bit red and patchy, but I could tell he would be a good looking guy one day. He was crouched in the stairwell of the rattan shop, playing cards with the other trike drivers.

When we stopped in front of Baby's, I told him to wait. Javier had played chauffeur for me many times, so I trusted him. Besides, I told him I'd pay extra if he stayed. He might have been sixteen, but he already knew not to turn down extra money.

Five minutes later, I walked out with my shopping list for next week and over 200 USD profit in my pocket.

After about a month of working for Baby, she asked me to up the ante a bit.

She wanted non-perishables. Hard goods.

"You get me two Sony cassette players, one Canon AT1 camera." She said as if she was asking for another can of Spam, at the same time handing me the money.

Food, cigarettes, liquor, those were consumable. Cameras and cassette players weren't. We were held accountable for all of the things that we bought on base. How would I explain the disappearance of an expensive 35mm camera?

I hesitated.

"You no want to shop?" She snarled. "You make more money for camera. Big money."

"No, no, I want to," I said, but I wasn't sure how deep I should go into this 'shopping.' "I just need to think about it."

I had heard stories of wives who started in the business as soon as they got off the plane.

By the time they were shipped out, they had saved up enough cash to open legitimate businesses in the states. Of course, most of them weren't Americans. Everyone knows we don't save.

"No time for think. Buyer come tomorrow. You no like shopping, tell me now."

I could see her sweet cherub face turning into an angry puffball, and I knew if I chose not to get the camera and Sonys, I would never get work from her again. Bottom line. I needed the money.

The Canon netted me $155.00 by itself and the cassette players $32.00 each. They were easy to get off base because they were small, so I didn't even bother with the taxi. It was worth the risk. Besides, when it was time to go, I could always say the kids broke them or they were gifts.

As I became more proficient at my job, I needed a place to hide my secret money. The best place I could think of was with Lucy. None of my friends, especially Rose, would have believed I trusted her enough to have her keep over four thousand dollars in her room. Not only did I trust her, I told her to hide it from me, and not let me use it, even if I asked.

Housegirl Bank.

If it had been in my hands, or closet, I know it would have been spent and then I would have been in the same situation as when I started out.

Most folks would have called me crazy, and as I think back on it, I probably was. Burdened with having to keep thousands of dollars in her shoe on the top of the closet shelf, poor Lucy. It was more money than she could hope to make in 5, maybe 10 years. I hate to imagine what I would do if put in a position like that. To her credit though, she never took a cent that I could figure. Not one grubby little peso.

While I was earning money, Jessie spent all of her spare time at the gym. She said she was training to be the next Nadia Comaneci. She lived and breathed her gymnastics. At least she was living and breathing, that was far better than what I was doing. She was old enough to know what was going on and I wanted to have a heart-to-heart with her. I had to make sure she wasn't suffering from my choices, but she was never in the mood. Then one evening, the two of us were sitting at the kitchen table and she just started talking.

"I want to go the Olympics," she announced. "Coach said I am good enough if I really work at it."

She had tumbled and flipped for as long as I could remember.

"I know you can do it if you work very hard." I was happy she had a dream.

"Mom, you know I have a big problem. I can't do anything if we keep living like this." Her 13-year-old voice was sorrowful.

"What do you mean?" I asked.

"You are always crying or in your room, it's like you're not here. And Dad doesn't really pay attention. I love him and everything but he's sort of absent. Don't you think you'd be happier if you get a divorce?"

Most kids beg their parents to stay together, but she was begging me to leave.

"I'm working on it Jessie. Just not yet."

"Why not?" She pushed.

"Because there's no place to go. I don't have enough money for us to leave and start over." I thought it best to just tell the truth.

"We can go live with Mama and Daddy Pete."

"No, Jess. I'm not going back to Ohio. We can't live with them. I have to be able to take care of us, myself. Besides, if we leave now, you would have to change schools in the middle of the year and there might not even be a gymnastics center nearby."

"It's not fair." she wailed. "All my friends have happy parents."

Tears were mixing with her freckles and dropping one by one on the table.

"Jessie, I'm sorry. For now, we just need to stay here and do the best we can. When we go back to the states, I will get an apartment and I'll get a job. You'll see." I patted her head and stroked her hair. It always soothed her.

"Mom?" She took deep breaths through her tears. "Where is Harris?"

"He went back to the states." The words echoed through my brain long after I said them.

She ran to her room and slammed the door. The song, "Thriller," filled the house. Her floor routine music. The walls beside me pounded with every beat. She was burning it off.

Chapter 22

I had been waiting for a call from Rose. She and Lance were in the honeymoon stage and in the unwritten laws of girl friendship, when a marriage is new, you give your friend space. Girl talk has to take a backseat. I desperately wanted to hear from her though. She had been incommunicado for almost two months. Rose was the only person in the world I could talk to about Harris.

I tried to erase him from my life as much as possible so that I could function. But what I really needed was someone who knew what I was going through.

Staying with Mike was a necessity, but I hated it more each day. I'm not proud to admit this, but I know I made him pay with my wrath for the loss of Harris.

Harris gave love with no strings. My mother's love had strings attached. Lots of them. They were all based on how good I made her look to her buddies. If I excelled in school, then I was wonderful and lovely. The most adorable daughter anyone could ever hope for. But if I became sullen or opinionated, which I frequently did, I was the most despicable child on Earth.

"How could you do this to me?" was the usual response to my public temper tantrums. My father was no better. They were a united front. Usually, against me.

Mike's 'love' was based on how well I entertained his troops or how good I looked when we went out. Of course, I never did meet his expectations. Mostly because the truth of it was he didn't want a short, curvy brunette with curly hair, he wanted the long-leggy blonde. He wanted something I could never be and I never did live it down. He even left for months when I was pregnant with Dana because I was too fat. Imagine nine months pregnant and too fat. How horrible of me. To pay him back, I called her Dana Siobhan, the name I originally wanted, even though we had agreed on Susan Michelle. But I figured if he didn't show up for her birth, he forfeited naming rights.

To think about it, I never truly felt I had anyone on my side until Harris. With him out of the picture, my loyalties were limited to my kids and one other person—*me*. I made a couple of vows to myself that year.

The first was to make enough money to get out with my kids and my self-respect. If I had to stay two more years in the Philippines to do it, I would bite my tongue and do my wifely duties, knowing that freedom was around the corner. The second was for Harris. I vowed that as long as I lived I would never love another man the way I loved him. What we had was brought to us from a heavenly realm. It was eternal. I had betrayed his love for me once and I was not going to do it again by giving what we had to someone else.

Even with that vow, I was still forced to play wife to Mike. And Mike had plans that we were going to repair the mess of a marriage we had and make it whole. Personally, I don't think you can make something whole that never had enough pieces to fit together in the first place. Regardless, he said he'd made up his mind we were going to stay together and that was final.

Thursday after Easter break, he acted on that attempt to pretend we had a real marriage. He decided that we could take a family trip to Grande—a little outpost island used by the Air Force and Navy personnel off the coast of Illongopo. It was the type of place listed in those travel books as a 'natural paradise.' Words like *rustic* and *charming* came to mind. Words like *isolated* and *desolate* seemed to apply as well. To get to Grande Island, we rode a bus to Manila and rented a car and driver to Subic Bay, which should have taken about six hours. But with a Filipino driving, it actually took less than four. Once there, we still had to board a tin-can boat that hopped bumpity-bump for two hours over to the island. The girls leapt with joy at the thought of adventure. I was happy just to leave Clark for a while.

We arrived at our cabin late in the afternoon to find there was no restaurant, no store, nowhere to entertain the girls indoors, and by then it was too late to go out to the beach.

Jessie kept bugging me about swimming, but the guy at the welcome desk warned us that they had just been inundated with jellyfish recently and almost everyone who went into the water had been stung. With nothing to do, the girls and I made the best of things by playing silly games like hide and seek. When it was Dana's turn, she chose the bathhouse by the cabin and thanks to her screams, she was a cinch to find.

"AHHHHHHHHHHHHHHHHHHHH."

Her yells were not in fun. They were fits of terror.

Jessie and I rushed in to find her face to face with a lizard that was probably as long as she was tall.

"Geez. That is the biggest thing I have ever

seen.," Jessie yelled as I grabbed her and stood back far enough to look at him from a safe distance.

"Mommy," whispered Dana, "We've got to get out of here."

The three of us ran like crazed animals. Out of the bathroom, though the grass, and back to the cabin in a sprint that would have made any track star proud. We spilled out the story of the lizard in less than a breath. Mike had been drinking San Miguel and watching a game on TV when we burst into the room.

I think, but I can't be certain, that the final straw came when I breathlessly said we needed to go back to the mainland.

From that point on, everything happened so fast.

I was simply thinking we needed some provisions and things for the kids to do like maybe a magazine for Jessie, and a coloring book for Dana. I knew the last boat left at 1930 PM and returned at 2130. It was already 1845 and I was in a rush.

I didn't expect what happened next as it had never happened before, but when I tried to pull Mike off the couch to get his attention, I vaguely remember a piercing pain that shot through my eye, and the next thing I knew, three MPs were standing over me getting ready to load me onto a stretcher.

I had no chance to think about what hit me because Dana was screaming, Jessie was packing bags and when I finally was able to focus, I saw Mike in handcuffs at the door being escorted out by two very serious looking military police.

Instead of going to get rations, I got a trip to the emergency ward and eight stitches in the side of my face to boot.

Mike was moved out of the house before the girls and I even reached Clark. Thanks to the Uniformed Code of Military Justice, it really is an offense to pop your wife in the face and cause a gash half the size of a dollar bill.

Two days later, I got a visit from the base chaplain.

"You'll need to make a decision quickly," he said. "Of course, they won't let Captain Holden back in the house until you are out, or until you agree to mandatory counseling, but they can only hold him in the brig for a week."

Here we go, again.

I gave up and called Rose. I relieved to hear that her voice was strong and clear. She agreed with me. The time had come. I didn't love him, and he only wanted me to stay to save face.

"Besides," said Rose, "Now you'll be free to find Harris. Where did you say he was going after he got out of the Air Force? San Diego?"

"No. His brother lives in San Diego. He said

he was going to move to Seattle."

"Well you should move to Seattle then." "No, Rose," was all I said.

I didn't have a reason not to move there, I just thought I would do this on my own and that meant my own city. Not a city where Harris or Mama or Daddy Pete or anyone I knew lived.

"Well, at least you know how to find him," she answered.

When the chaplain called back for my decision, I had two words for him.

"I'll leave."

Those two words started the paper ball rolling and before I knew it, movers were packing my furniture in brown wrap and peanuts. All the lovely wicker that I had handpicked, or in some cases designed, had to be divided between me and Mike. It was little consolation that half of everything belonged to him when I was the one who would have to go out and figure out how to make a life for the three of us with nothing but my bootleg profits to fall back on.

Funny thing about leaving the bosom of the military. There's no cushion. I fell short of my ten-year mark, but after being punched in the face I wasn't about to wait for it no matter what the cost. Of course, they make the guy pay child support. That was at least a given. But beyond that, I was on my own.

For a dependent wife, as soon as the tie is broken, even with eight stitches and a gash that would forever stay as reminder, it's all over. Officially, I was still a military dependent until the divorce, but unofficially, I was nothing. I could use the base in the states for medical. I could even go to the commissary and BX, but was there any repatriation help? Did I get a check so that I could settle down in my new city without worrying about where money for food was coming from until I got a job?

What I had, was my two years worth of savings from Housegirl Bank and hopes that I would be able to make it for the first time in my life.

As much as I wanted to start over, I was scared and remorseful. Guilt over the things I had done to get me to this place. If there had been no Harris…or if I had really tried harder with Mike. I couldn't blame him for everything anymore. Mike wasn't all bad. I held responsibility in this drama, too.

As Padi Ko taxi pulled up to the house to collect us, I promised myself I wouldn't cry. Lucy hugged the kids hard and started to sob loudly. Before we drove away, all of us were taking our last look through tears. I remember Lucy's eyes. The lost look. I found her a job with one of the single Air Force women on base because I couldn't think of leaving her with no place to go and no source of income. I hoped she would be happy in her new home.

I never thought I would cry so much leaving a place. I certainly didn't do that when we took off at Travis for the PI. I didn't even bring a tear to the surface when I left Columbus and watched as my family disappeared from view.

But in my window seat on the Flying Tiger, I couldn't hold back the tears. Dana had stopped crying, and even though she felt grown up at eight, she was eagerly checking out the 'flight pack' the stewardess gave her on the way in. Jessie had done most of her crying when she said goodbye to Lucy. I, on the other hand, could only think of Harris and Rose and how living in this steamy, bug infested country had been the best thing that had ever happened to me. As the plane took off down the runway, I knew that I would never have the feelings I felt here, or the sense of wonder. But it wasn't until we flew above the base on our way to California that I understood the loss. Harris was gone. Rose was gone. Now I had gone, too.

Part 2

Chapter 23

What I really wanted was for someone to come and rescue me. I wanted a hand to hold. But the only hands I held were young and they needed me most of all. No one was going to take up the slack for me this time. No mom, no pop, or husband to come to my aid. I had made this journey and decided to take it like a woman, but secretly, I feared it was going to be the end of me.

Most of the money I saved in the PI I used to get an apartment in a really nice neighborhood. The place was far more than I could afford, but I remember my dad once said, "You can be the poorest person in the best neighborhood but never be the smartest person in a bad neighborhood."

I was beginning to understand his point. I wanted my kids to go to good schools and have friends that came from good families. I wanted them to have a chance for a real education.

After all, they had been to Korea and Hong Kong and the Ginza in Tokyo. Most American kids couldn't say that. I knew they wouldn't fit with the low life in neighborhoods I could afford. So I spent my last few dollars on an apartment nestled by a hillside and I went in search of a job.

That is when I started the if-onlying. If only I had gone to college and finished. If only I had a trade. If only I could work in a fast food restaurant and not feel bad about it. (Thank God, it never came to that.) I could do clerical work. At least, that's what all the temp agencies told me…until I did their typing test and they realized that I took three times longer than anyone else to turn out a one-page letter. Or, I could go crawling back to the place from whence I came. No, not Ohio, but the Air Force base. And luckily, when you part from the USAF, that is exactly where they dump you and your furniture. On another base. Then you have to crawl off on your own, any way you can.

Since I was married to Mike for the time being, I still held that pink ID card. And in the states, it made me first in line for a job because unlike overseas, military spouses in America got top priority.

Just like the Beverly Hillbillies, I thought Southern California was the place to be. So when they asked me back at Clark where I wanted my 'household goods' to go, I said March Air Force Base. It occupied a little pit of a town about 60 miles outside Los Angeles, and if it hadn't been for the base, there would have been no reason for that town to exist.

Moreno Valley wasn't exactly LA, and LA was just too darn far away to even think of trying to get a job there, so I moved just far enough from base to be in that good neighborhood. Then, without missing a beat, I turned right around and headed back to March Air Force Base BX. They were looking for a gift wrapper. The official job title was listed as customer service representative to make it sound impressive. At minimum wage, it did need something to impress me, but a job was a job, and I was hired to do it. So I put on my finest handmade Filipina dress and drove my VW Bug (which had deflated my funds) straight to the base where I worked wrapping presents. Mostly, I was wrapping stuff for single guys who bought gifts for their dates, or for married women who were getting birthday or anniversary presents for a husband who you just knew wasn't going to reciprocate.

Jessie still knew one day she'd be going to the Olympics and to prove it, she was up at dawn so I could drive her to practice before and after school. Then one day, while I was at work,

I got a phone call. The kind no parent wants to hear when her kids are out of sight.

"Mrs. Holden? This is the ER nurse at Riverside Community Hospital. Your daughter Jessie was injured in an accident at her gymnastics practice today. She had a pretty serious fracture, but she will be fine. Still, you should probably come as soon as possible."

She didn't have to say another word. I was cashing out my drawer and picking up my car keys all at the same time.

Poor Jessie looked like the tiny baby she was years ago when she fell off of the bed doing one of her famous back flips. It was hard to see her flat on the gurney as they wheeled her off to X-ray.

"Do you…think…my leg…will…get better?" she managed through the sobs.

"It will be fine, Jessie. Don't worry."

But a compound fracture of the femur meant she was in shock and had to have surgery, and I wasn't so sure that 'fine' was the appropriate word.

Six months with a cast and physical therapy still didn't bring her leg back to its former flexibility.

In the orthopedist's office, we sat there silently waiting to hear the news. I looked around at the models of knees and spinal columns, but I was only concerned about one thing. Jessie's leg.

Jessie's fingers were shaking as she tried to steady them by grasping the sides of the wooden chair. I reached over to hold her hand, and she gave me a look of pure terror.

As the doctor entered the room, her face said it all.

"I have been going over the MRI and the X-rays and everything looks pretty good. Jessie, you should be able to continue normal activities without any disability. But...."

And there it was. The 'but' that I knew was coming.

"I really can't see you going back to competitive gymnastics. Your leg is never going to be as strong as it was before the accident, and the danger of reinjuring it precludes the strenuous exercise involved in an Olympic bid. I'm sorry Jessie, but that is the situation. Of course, you can do some gymnastics, but the long hours of practice you did before the accident are not wise. If you were to reinjure that leg, I couldn't promise a positive outcome the second time."

Jessie hung her head and cried harder than I had ever seen her cry before.

We left the office in silence. I didn't know how to make it better, and Jessie didn't want me to try.

As the weeks ticked by, Jessie first decided

she never wanted to see a gymnastics meet again. Then slowly, she began watching the kids at the gym as they went through their routines.

"Jessie, you don't have to keep going back if you don't want to." I tried to be sympathetic to her pain.

But Jessie was far stronger than me, and she returned to the scene of the crime to face it the way she had done everything. Head on, with dignity.

She seemed satisfied with the fact that she was good enough to teach gymnastics, and the fact that they even paid her a little bit for doing so made it even better.

For months, coaching and high school occupied her while she worked on a new future. Lots of ideas crossed her mind that year, so when she came home with a flyer about auditioning for a TV show in LA, I didn't pay much attention. But I had forgotten what it was like to be a teenager. Just when I thought I had her all figured out, she'd turn on a dime.

"I've always wanted to be an actress," said Jessica.

"How come you never told me this before?" I was completely caught off guard.

"How could I be an actress in the Philippines?"

She had a point. This was the first time she

actually had the chance to do it.

"Yeah but Jess, you have to be really serious about this, 'cause it means driving for an hour and a half each way."

"I swear, Mom, I want it more than I have ever wanted anything in my whole life."

Her *whole life* at that point amounted to 16 years. And so far, we had gone through guitar, ballet, ice-skating and gymnastics. I admit, I tended to indulge these notions, but she played a reasonable guitar, she danced like a pro, could have been a competitive ice skater if we hadn't moved to the PI, and gymnastics, well, in my heart, I knew she would have been Olympic material if she hadn't cracked that leg.

If acting was the thing that would replace gymnastics, I couldn't refuse.

Chapter 24

We trotted off in brake-grinding traffic to get Jessie to the audition along with about a hundred other parents and children. The auditorium was packed with wall-to-wall hopefuls. Even though it was a Wednesday night, kids filled every open spot on the floor. They were doing math homework and writing paragraphs for history papers. Each one waited a turn to spend all of three minutes inside the door at the end of the line. I felt like I had stumbled into a whole subculture that I never knew existed. Four hours later, weary from my efforts to keep Dana from being bored, Jessie emerged from the door with no expression and no words. An hour and a half later, we were back at home.

"What happened?" I asked.

Jessie shrugged.

"What did they ask you?" I tried to pry some information out of her.

"You know, like my name, and age and stuff."

"No, Jess I don't know. I've never been to a Hollywood audition."

"Why are you getting mad at me?"

"I'm not," I said, although I could feel my irritation growing. "I just want to know what they do, and what they asked you to do."

"Mom, just forget it. I didn't do very well, and they knew it was my first audition. I didn't have the right pictures, or anything. And they said I needed a resume." She started sniffling. "I didn't even know how to say my own name right."

Obviously, there was protocol to this 'Hollywood' business that we weren't aware of.

So when the phone rang Thursday afternoon for a callback, I was in shock. I picked Jess and Dana up from school and ran straight to the Riverside Public Library to find all the books I could about Hollywood and acting, and how you go about getting into the business. I took the only two books they had and began devouring them. I had less than an hour to figure out what kind of resume a teenager could possibly have and what it meant to 'slate your name.'

This time when we arrived at the 'interview' (I found out *audition* was a word outsiders use), the numbers had dwindled significantly. Only about thirty or forty kids were scattered around the huge room. Again, homework was spread out on the floor, but each child was behind the door longer. Some almost fifteen or twenty minutes. That had to be a good sign. So when it was Jessica's turn, I started counting. Five, ten, eleven, twelve, thirteen. The door opened and out walked Jessie. She was smiling. I tried not to say a word or make any kind of expression until we got to the car.

"Well?," I asked.

"Mom, I got it."

We all started screaming.

"I can't believe it. I am going to be on TV. Can *you* believe it?"

The tides had turned. Fortune had smiled. Jessie was going to be in a Hollywood show. We didn't know anything about the show, but we knew she was going to be in it and that was enough.

The next day, I got the details. George Wellington, the Academy Award winning actor, had decided to do a show for kids, and he wanted them to be able to do acrobatics and dance. Jessie, of course, was a natural choice. But it turned out that she wasn't a lead or even a featured performer. She was one of the background gymnasts. An extra.

Jessie was paid an extra's salary, and I used

more than that in gas just getting her back and forth to rehearsals. But like everything else she tried, she was good. And with a taste of Hollywood under her belt, she was determined to become an actress.

She was aglow with possibilities. It was something I wanted to feel. Maybe it was close to what I felt when we first arrived at Clark. Or when I first saw Harris, or even the day Rose told me I could take courses on base.

The desire she had to be an actress got all of us, even Dana, talking about 'headshots' and 'sides.'

There were agents and photos and lessons and resumes. And then there were scam artists who knew just how to take your money and give you false hope. I was too poor to get caught in that trap, so I had to arm myself with enough knowledge to keep from getting ripped off.

Jessie's dream took me away from my obsessive thoughts and longings for Harris, and the worry of how I was going to support my girls. That dream of hers was powerful enough to keep me working towards something.

Even still, I never had any peace for long, because in the back of my mind dollar signs just kept adding up and flying away from me. Money was tight. I couldn't afford the long-distance calls to Rose. When I did make them, I regretted it because the bill came at the end of the month and I was in trouble. I was always in trouble. But I called her anyway. I'd never had a friend before who I truly missed. If they were there, then that was great, but when they left, oh well. No looking back. No goodbyes. No need to hang on to the past. I just moved on from everything and everyone I knew.

But the Philippines had changed all of that because I missed Rose almost as much as I missed Harris. I couldn't imagine them not in my life. So I spent more money than I should have and I called her. We had made a deal. First it would be my turn, then hers until one week when it was her turn, and nothing. I waited for days, but when there was still no call, I dialed and got Lance.

He told me what I guess I already knew.

"Her kidneys failed, Leah. She's in the hospital on dialysis."

My hands trembled at the news. I tried to picture Rose hooked up to a machine.

"What about a transplant?," I asked.

"Her name went on the list last week. I don't know how long it takes. But, don't worry. For now, she is okay. They put in a shunt to get her stable."

"What about her sister? She said her sister might do it."

"Yeah, that's something we are going to

look at. There is a lot to think about right now." He sounded tired. "And there is JJ to think about, too."

"Of course. Can I call the hospital?"

"There's no phone in the room. She's at the base hospital."

"Well, tell her I called, Lance."

"Of course, I will."

"And tell her I love her."

"Leah? Don't worry, she'll be okay."

Chapter 25

The Riverside Public Library was not exactly the place to find out about Hollywood. I kept looking for books like: *How to Get Your Child in Show Business*; *How to Become a Paid Actor*; *How to Work in Commercials*; and *How to Model in Magazines*. I finally asked the librarian on duty for help. I hate to stereotype, but honestly, she could have been plucked right out of a film role, herself. Little horn-rimmed glasses sticking to her nose and all.

"Oh, Honey," she said in that practiced quiet voice that all librarians have acquired. "You will never find that type of thing here. You need to go to Hollywood, There's a bookstore called Samuel French. That's where my cousin went before she got into the business. She danced in a movie with Patrick Swayze, did I already tell you that? It's the only place I know of where you can get that kind of information."

It was beginning to seem like 'the business' was some type of sorority or mafia. You had to be made a member. Folks like us couldn't just go and say, "Hey there, I want to be an actor, put me on your list." You had to have the 'in' connections, the hook up.

Obviously, we had none of that. But I did have a Bug that could get me from Moreno Valley to Hollywood, so on Saturday morning, I packed up the three of us and we made our journey into the land of movie stars, shiny cars, and agents ready to sign up the latest child actor standing on every corner.

Well, that was what I thought anyway.

"This place is gross," yelled Dana from her seat in the little luggage area at the very back of the Bug. Dana wasn't much for bad neighborhoods, and being a suburban type of girl, lower Sunset Blvd was way too seedy for her taste.

"Quiet," I snapped back. I was trying to read the map and make turns all at the same time.

"But I don't like it here. It's ugly."

I had to admit, what I had seen of Sunset Blvd didn't do much for me, either. But this was where we had to go to get to Samuel French and by God, this is where we were going. It was not a vacation. It was a mission.

"Dana, give me a break, I'm looking for this

place. Hold on."

"Oh, my God." Now it was Jessie's turn. "Did you *see* that?"

I kept my eyes on the street signs. She didn't continue.

"What is it?" I asked.

"How do I know what it was?" said Jessica. "I think it was a guy dressed up in a mini skirt. Mom maybe Dana's right, do you know where you are?"

Well of course I didn't. But that was neither here nor there.

"You know, I could use a little help here," I said.

"But you don't know where we are, and you don't know where we are going," said Jessie.

"I'm doing the best I can, Jessie. I have a map and the address.... It looks like we can't be too far away now. Besides, we've been tons of places we didn't know where we were, so this isn't new stuff.

"Yeah, but it never looked as bad as it does here," said Jessie.

"Yeah, I'm scared," Dana whined.

"Well, I am not asking you to live here Dana, I'm only going to the bookstore and then we can go straight home. And if you would just calm down and relax a bit, you might even find it's fun."

If I could have relaxed a bit we would have had more fun is what I was really saying. Not that I was scared of Hollywood or drag queens, but we were all out of our element. And the kids knew it.

When I finally found the famous store, I picked out two thick books, for a grand total of $44.95. One, which the guy behind the counter, (a definite wannabe actor, himself) said was 'the bible' of how to break into acting.

Once we were home, safe in our little suburban apartment, I started devouring the books. I didn't stop until late into the night. All of the things that needed to be done, places that I needed to contact. How to find an agent. Why we couldn't do it without one. Who the *real* agents were. Where to get the *right* headshots. Boy, was there ever a lot to do in this acting business.

The big surprise was that the money involved to get started was minimal if you knew what you were doing. But I had been talking to all the wrong people. Ones that lived in Riverside and San Bernardino and Pomona. Those folks thought you could have a movie career living out in the boonies, working with local 'agents,' But there were no *real* agents out there. If you wanted to get into the movies, or TV commercials you could only go one place: Hollywood.

And, you couldn't just go to Hollywood on the weekends, you had to *be* in Hollywood, or someplace darn close. Because agents didn't call on the weekends, they called at 10 AM on a Tuesday morning with an interview at a casting studio for 3:00 that same afternoon. And they didn't care if you were 7 or 73. As soon as school was over for the day, rushes of kids started making the rounds with very little time to get from one place to another.

I got the picture. If Jessie was seriously going to do this, we had some decisions to make. Serious ones.

That night, I called a Holden family meeting and laid out the options.

"You guys, I've really been thinking about this Hollywood thing. It's kind of a problem."

I could see Jessie's face fall.

"No, Jessie, I'm not saying we can't do it, but I'm telling you we can't do it from here. It won't work. So if you are sure about this, I think we should just plan to finish out the school year and then move over to the Hollywood area so that we are able to get you to interviews and get an agent for you. But that means you have to be *very* serious because it's a big move."

"Me too?," asked Dana.

"Of course you can move with us." I laughed. "You can even act if that is what you want".

"Mommmmmmm." screeched Dana.

"But Mom, I am already an actress. So why do I have to move?"

"Jessie, you got a job in *The Bear Run,* but that doesn't make you an actress. It's a start. It gives you a credit. If that is what you want then we can stay and you can do some more stuff like that here and there. I don't know—you have to tell me. What do *you* want to do with this acting thing?"

"You know what I want, Mom...I want to be an actress on TV. And I want to do movies."

"Then that is what I am telling you. You have to do it the right way. You can't just find acting jobs in the paper. It doesn't work like that."

"So we are moving to Hollywood?"

"Well not necessarily Hollywood." I realized by then nobody actually lives in Hollywood if they can live somewhere else. "But close enough to be able to get to the places where you can have a chance to be the actor you want to be."

Jess and Dana started jumping up and down and screaming and twirling around chanting, "We're moving to Hollywood. We're moving to Hollywood."

By late evening, every kid on the block had heard that Dana and Jessica were destined to be famous actresses and we were moving to Hollywood. Or at least close.

Chapter 26

Until the move, I still had to work at the base, but with a paycheck like mine, there was no extra money to call Okinawa and cover my expenses. Twice in six months the phone was cut off and since it was the least of the necessities, it had to go.

Okay, I did spend money on dance lessons, headshots and resumes. Along with the rent, gas, and food, there just wasn't enough to go around. The $154.00 a month from Mike certainly went far to fill the void in my income. Or at least that is what *he* thought.

At first, when the girls needed something, I would call him and ask, no, beg, for some help. But I knew he really thought his responsibility began and ended with that government issued $154.00. I soon found out that I was looking weak and getting nowhere by asking for help. Advice on the subject came from all directions.

"Leah, you need to sue him. Take him to

court." That was my mother.

"Don't let him get away with it...yous didn't make em by yourself." Rose.

"What's wrong with you? You guys are starving and he doesn't even think he has any reason to contribute to his own children's welfare? Go to the child support agency. Turn him in." My sister.

All of them were well intentioned, but the truth is, I just didn't have the steam in me to start or continue the fight it would have taken to get Mike in front of a judge. I had been through quite enough with him and was happy to be out of the marriage. The last thing I wanted was to see him or even hear his voice again.

I had fought the good fight with him and lost. What was left of me needed to be looking in another direction. Not backwards towards Mike and Clark Air Base. It might have been stupid on my part, but I didn't even want his money unless it came gift wrapped without a note.

What I wanted was Harris. With his brother in San Diego I figured it wouldn't be hard to track him down. His brother had a more unusual name than Michael. Colin Harrison. I was sure there weren't too many of them in the telephone book if he happened to be listed.

I called long distance information, 555-1212.

"What city and state?"

"San Diego, California"

"Thank you. What is the listing?"

"Colin Harrison"

"Thank you. One moment please"

"I have two listings. One on 45th St. and one on Mission Camino Blvd."

I had no idea which one might be Harris's brother.

"Could I have them both please?"

"Certainly. The first one on 45th St. is 619-555-7782. The other is 619-555-8251.

I looked at the numbers and started to dial. Then I waited. I didn't want to go back to Harris like this. I didn't want him to see me broke, struggling, needing him for support, monetary support that is. I wanted to show him that I was the person he had faith in when we were together. He used to tell me that I would make it on my own and I was smart and strong, and I wouldn't need Mike.

But I hadn't proven that to myself or anyone else yet. My still frazzled ends weren't meeting. Each month, I was getting more and more behind. I had even gone to the state welfare department to apply for food stamps. This was not the way I had dreamed of reuniting with Harris.

So I tucked away the two numbers in the back of my desk drawer. Inside a book, one that

Harris had given me. The one that had a picture of the man with the kindly face on the cover.

Autobiography of a Yogi. It was all I had left from Harris, so I held on to it for dear life. I read it more than once, and I don't know why, but each time, it made me feel a tiny bit stronger.

Maybe it was time to read it again.

Chapter 27

When I had a phone that worked, I talked to Rose more often than I should have.

Her voice got froggy at times. On those days, our conversations would be short and I could tell she was getting winded. But, once in a while, we spent over an hour on the phone together just laughing at the things we did and how we got from the land of bananas and Nipa huts to our new lives, mine back in the states and hers in Okinawa.

She talked a lot about Lance and how he was the best thing that had ever happened to her, and how she couldn't believe he was still there even though she was so sick.

"I know Juan wouldn't have been able to handle this, Leah. That is why God gave me Lance."

"Remember, you knew he was the one as soon as you saw him?"

"I did know, didn't I? Just like you and

Harris."

"Yeah" I answered, but in my heart, I knew it wasn't like me and Harris. Rose had Lance and they were together. She noticed the silence.

"Soo, have you heard from him?"

"No."

"Well, he was hurt pretty bad. Lance said he talked to some of the guys after the whole thing happened...you know...he was in bad shape, Leah. He even talked about killing himself. I didn't want to tell you, but it wasn't easy for him, either. Now that you're back and you're getting a divorce, it's different. You can call him."

"Not yet, Rose. I can't call him until I get my life straightened out."

"Are you Loca? The man loved...loves you. He won't give a crap about whether your life is straight or not. Look at Lance, if I waited to have my life straightened out, I would never be with him, 'cause this is about as straight as it gets for me."

"I have his brother's number in San Diego. At least I think it's his brother's number."

"Well, shit. Call him."

"Yeah, I will."

But no matter what Rose said to me, pride was not going to let me do it before I felt the time was right. And, truthfully, I was scared. What if he didn't want to talk to me again?

What if I had done too much damage?

"Hey Loca?" Rose interrupted my thought. "Just remember that whatever happens was meant to be."

"Yeah, I know, Rose."

I wasn't sure whether she was talking about her or me.

Three days later, the phone rang. It was Lance. Rose collapsed when her dialysis shunt became infected. She was in the hospital again, but this time it didn't look so good.

"I know she would want you to be here, Leah."

"I want to come, but you know I can't. I have the kids and there is no money." I felt like I was letting her down when she needed me most.

He could hear me trying to hold back the tears.

"It's okay Leah, she might not even know if you were here. She is pretty sick."

"Lance, I don't know what to say."

"I don't, either."

When the tears started in earnest, I couldn't hold back. I spent the evening curled up on the bed with the muted TV for company. Thank God, it was the weekend. When Jess and Dana wanted to know why I was crying, I just told them Rose was sick, but Jessie was smart enough to understand that sick wasn't the extent of it.

"Is she going to die, Mom?"

All I said was, "I don't know."

Even though she was powerless to help me, Jessie pulled a blanket around us both and hugged me tight. Dana didn't know exactly what was wrong, but she joined in, too.

That night, we fell asleep huddled together with nothing but the tick tock of my old travel clock as background noise. It had a soothing rhythm that played like a mantra.

Two weeks before we made the big move, my divorce papers arrived. Signed, sealed and delivered. I didn't expect the jubilation I felt. They spelled the end of Mike and the beginning of my final freedom. We had been together for over 16 years and we were still eight months short of the 10 years married to give me permanent military spouse status. It was a tough way for it to end. After all the time I had put in not to get part of that pension. But I was so happy it was over, I didn't really care. Nor did I think about the consequences of getting the papers signed early.

None of Rose's admonishments about doing her time and waiting until that magic 10 worked on me. I just wanted my freedom and the sooner, the better. So as I read my new name, Leah Conners, which was actually my old name, I rejoiced. I was a single woman, again. Just a little more to do and then I could call Harris. I would confess what I had done and more importantly, why. Hopefully, armed with the truth, my actions wouldn't seem so unthinkable and I would be able to start anew with him by my side. That was the dream I had each night as I soothed myself to sleep.

When all of our PI furniture was finally packed up and settled into the U-HAUL truck, I reveled in the fact that I had chosen my furniture well. With no man on the scene to help with the move, and no one bigger than me to push things from the 2nd floor apartment to the truck, it was a good thing that I had purchased lightweight rattan with removable cushions. The only item to cause me any trouble at all was the fridge, and that was actually not as much of a challenge as I figured it would be.

I watched people move in and out of that apartment building in Riverside all year, so I knew just what to do. If you lift up the refrigerator and stick an old blanket about halfway under, then set the fridge down on it and push, when you finally get the whole thing on top of the blanket, you just take it for a ride...carefully down the stairs, then up the ramp and onto the truck.

It may sound impossible for a 5′ 2″ woman and two young girls to pull off alone, but darned if it didn't work. I think I had as much pride in being able to move that furniture as I did in trying to make a life for myself.

"Man? What man? We don't need no man....We don't need no man." I was chanting it without even realizing that sound was coming out of my mouth. Soon, the kids were chanting, too.

"Man, what man? We don't need no man."

Total time of the move was four hours and 36 minutes and we were on the road. This time to make our mark in TV and movies. We were moving to the San Fernando Valley. Just north of Hollywood and halfway to the stars.

Chapter 28

The 'Valley' wasn't really so different from the valley we left. We drove past the same scenery for 60 miles. Strip malls, real malls, towns blending into towns, no barriers to mark where one left off and the other began. It was no greener, no hillier, nor was it much more luxurious, not the part where we moved anyway, but it was the place to live if you wanted to be in show business.

In my best impression of what a responsible adult does, a couple weeks earlier I had scouted out this very tiny apartment in Studio City. Even the name was pleasing to the ear. From the sound, you'd think it was row-to-row Hollywood studios. And there were a couple of well-hidden ones. But mostly, it was strip malls, 7-Elevens and thousands of apartment buildings styled only the way LA can build them. The typical complex had between 12 to 20 units with a dirty, leaf-filled swimming pool in the center. Regardless of the lack of taste, which I attributed to 1960s architecture, anything in Studio City couldn't be all that bad. So even though it was the ugliest, smallest, most disgusting color orange apartment that looked like a Motel 6, and it only had one bedroom, I took it. Because once again, the rule was: If you move to the worst building in the best neighborhood you can afford, then at least you are in the right zip code. In other words, if you live in a garage, you know that's not a good thing (though I think it has some coolness factor). But if the garage has the zip of 90210, then as shallow as it seems, you have arrived.

Our apartment had white walls. All apartments have white walls. I know everyone doesn't love bright, neon color like me, but why does it have to be the whitest white possible? Couldn't they put in a dash of blue just to soften the glare? When we arrived and started placing furniture, I found out just how tiny the bedroom was. Barely large enough to hold two twin beds and a large dresser.

After living in separate rooms all their lives, the girls thought their shared 8x10 box was equivalent to the State Penitentiary. Jessica, of course, was number one on the 'I hate everything about it, and it's all your fault' bandwagon. But I reminded her why we were making the move in the first place, and that was the end of that little drama.

I got the living room as my bedroom. I usually fell asleep watching the TV no matter what room I was in, so I could just get a pull-out futon and go on about my business as if it were something I did on purpose, not something I had to do since I couldn't afford any better.

Dana's first day of school proved I was out of my league. Cars came in different varieties at different locales and at this school, VWs were out and Mercedes, BMWs and Saabs were in. The crowd let out and kids of all sizes stampeded for the parked cars. I saw Dana walking with a little girl about her same height. She had big news.

"Mom, guess what? Some of the kids in my class are actors. You know the girl on *Putting It Straight?* She is in *my* class."

"I imagine lots of kids around here are in the industry," I said.

"Yeah, and you know that girl I was talking to just now? She has been in about a zillion commercials. McDonald's, and Tide, and you know the one with the kid who cries cause her mother won't buy her a Barbie doll? That's her."

Now I knew why that girl looked familiar.

"But you will never guess who else goes to my school? Of course, they are little so they're not in my grade, I think they are in kindergarten. The Handie Twins."

I could tell she was feeling like a celebrity herself just because she went to school with those children. I was glad she was happy with our move.

I knew I had taken a huge leap of faith this time. Quitting my work at the BX and moving west. I didn't even have a job in the valley. No money at all in fact, other than child support in that amount I never stopped complaining about, so I tucked my tail and went on welfare, not just for food stamps this time, but for the medical and a check as well. I was confident it wouldn't be long before the situation changed.

The week after my first check arrived, I saw an ad in the Sunday paper:

Wanted: Call reps for major television production. Need several for graveyard shift. Pay and benefits. Contact SAR Productions at 555-2398.

Not just a job, but one that involved show business. The name of the program was *Crime Calls*. Each night, they featured unsolved crimes and invited viewers to contact the station after the show if they had any information to help solve the crime. I was hired to be one of the voices on the other end. A room full of us were actually on the other end, so the place was divided into cubicles and the chatter of 20 people all talking at the same time constantly filled the air. But the money was way better than I had ever earned before and the hours were great. I was happy to take the midnight shift and with Jessica being 15, I let the girls stay alone while I worked. Besides, she would have laughed at me had I suggested they have a sitter.

Sometimes, I slept in the day, but I can't really recall when. Most of the time, I was dog eared and tired because I had to hurry home in the morning and get Dana ready for school. Graveyard had its advantages. Still, the late shift was not for the weak willed. All the loons came out at night. To prove the theory that the moon has an effect on people and their behavior, just like clockwork, when a full moon rose, so did the calls and the psychos stepped up their assaults.

A very insistent woman who swore she had seen a suspect at the local 7-Eleven was one of our lunar callers.

"Ma'am, where did you say this 7-Eleven is?," I asked

"On the corner of Vineland and I'm here right now. You had better hurry. He is getting near the cashier."

"You mean the 7-Eleven in North

Hollywood? And what makes you think he is the suspect?"

"He is. I'm telling you he is the exact same person I saw on the reenactment last night."

"You mean the actor?"

"Oh. That was an actor?"

The big perk about working graveyard was that I had time to go on interviews with Jessie.

On one of those interviews, Jessie and I both had a win/win. We walked into the Carla Barter Agency at half-past one and while we were waiting for Jessie to go in for her appointment, I started talking away to the lady behind the desk. Asking her all types of questions about the agency.

"Are you SAG franchised? Do you have a breakdown computer? Who does your courier service? How many times a day do you send out headshots and resumes? What does your client list look like? Are you commercial or theatrical?"

Then she stopped me cold. I was sure I had blown it for Jessie.

"Young lady, are you interviewin' *me*?"

"Sorry, I guess I got carried away." I laughed. "I've been doing a lot of research on the business and I just never had anyone willing to answer all of my questions before."

"Well, I gotta tell ya', she said in her Texas drawl, "I like your spunk...haven't seen anything quite like it for long time."

I wondered if I had helped or hurt Jessie's chances.

"You know we don't really handle kids, but if ya wanta do this work, I think you'd be good at it. You'd have to work on commission, and get your own list of clients, but if you're interested, I'll give ya a break. You ever thought about being an agent?"

Had I thought about it? It had crossed my mind, oh, about five hundred thousand times. But mostly, what I thought about was paying the next grocery bill. It was an impractical proposal, but at the same time, maybe it was a good idea. I would be able to send Jessie out on anything I wanted, and what I didn't know I could learn. It wasn't nursing, but I *would* be in control of Jessie's future. Not only that, I would be a Hollywood agent. Now that had to have some clout somewhere. So, once again, I plunged ahead 'cause an opportunity like this doesn't knock more than once a century, and I hadn't time to wait for the next one.

"I would *love* it." I answered.

"Good. Then, come on in here and I'll show ya'll where your desk will be, and then you can have yourself a darlin little weekend and report to work on Monday morning."

"Thank you so much, you have no idea…Miss Ba…."

"Just call me Carla." She winked at me.

I wanted to scream. Soon as I hit the door, I made phone calls to everyone. With Rose doing better, of course she was first, but they all started the same way.

"You are never going to guess what happened to me today…."

Chapter 29

Second week on the job, I went over to RenMar studios to check on some of Carla's clients who had been hired to do a day shoot. I had no clients myself yet, other than Jessica and Dana, but Carla was "grooming" me and so she sent me tail wagging to any of the sets where they needed a body.

I cruised around Hollywood pretending in my head to be a big wheeler-dealer. Of course, I never would have admitted that to anyone else, but I was rather impressed with my new job title. Children's Talent Agent. It sounded so important.

And then just to bring my ego back down to Earth, I found out how much clout I had when I pulled up to the south gate in my Bug.

"You have a pass?" asked the guard.

"I'm from the Carla Barter Agency," I announced proudly.

"I don't care where you're from. If you

don't have a pass, you can't drive on the lot."

"I have clients working here, I have to get on the lot." I put on my most indignant face.

"Oh, you can come on. You'll just have to walk."

So that's how it went. Even in Hollywood. Agencies had reputations. If you were from one of the big ones, you had *carte blanche,* and that got you on any lot in town. I soon found out how small the agency I worked for was, and how little it had in the way of power. I got lots of exercise in those days. Walking on lots from parking areas two and three blocks from the actual studio. I didn't care though, because I was seeing TV shows produced, movies being made and commercials being shot.

Then one night at the call-in center, one of the ladies I worked with said to me, "I am so proud of you, you are such a strong woman."

I'm not sure why that sent me into a tailspin, but it did. I wasn't sure I knew what she meant.

Was I strong, because I didn't cry? Well, that was true, in public I didn't. I guess those days on end with covers pulled over my head don't count.

Or was it because I was raising my kids alone? That wasn't strength, that was necessity. Who else was going to do that for me?

I didn't feel strong at all. Maybe the real

answer was that I was too afraid not to be.

The word *strong* belonged to Rose.

But me, I deserved no awards because the truth is, when you really, seriously, have no one to rely on except yourself, somehow, I think most of us find the way.

Strength is a funny thing. You only get lauded with that label when you are living precariously. Nobody who is rich, famous, successful, or gets things easily in life is called *strong*. But, get an incurable disease, or work two jobs, or start out penniless and fight your way up…have no friends, no husband, no support…lose everything including hope. Ah, yes, okay, now you are strong.

And the whole time I was being "strong" I was cracking like the Titanic, post iceberg. I fantasized about Harris and Rose, and how it was when we all were taking classes at Wagner High.

Sometimes lying in bed, I stared at the ceiling, thinking how pathetic I was to be living in the past at my age. Mid-thirties and nothing but sadness to fill my nights. All my real life was in a country far, far away. With people who were no longer part of it, except in memory or a long distance call. What was going on now was just filler until Harris and I were reunited or life played itself out.

Chapter 30

I had just added three clients to my very own list. A little boy from El Salvador who everyone thought was Mexican; A big Mexican guy, who everyone thought was Asian; and a little girl from Riverside of all places, who had a voice that could fill up Radio City Music Hall.

I hate to say it, but as far as potential in Hollywood was concerned, they probably had more than Jessica. Being an objective agent and all, I had to think like that.

I remember meeting the mayor of Columbus once when I was a young girl. He did tours of the public schools and I thought he was the most famous person in the world. But as an agent, I was meeting people everyone had seen on the big screen and the little one, too.

I practically knocked over a whole stand of potato chips when Dana and I ran into those twins from her school at the neighborhood Stop-n-Shop. Although I loved every minute of being "Ms. Hollywood," I was a little too star struck for my own good.

Somewhere in the back of my mind, in the depths of my subconscious, I wondered if underlying all of my actions was the desire to just have my family and Harris be proud of me...or maybe to love me a bit more. I knew what kind of family I came from; it was love attached to goals and results. No matter what you did, you had to do more. No matter how smart you were, you had to be smarter. No matter how many times you succeeded, you were always reminded of the failures, first. I knew this life of TV and movies would win them bragging rights. Not many people in good old Columbus could say their daughter was a Hollywood agent.

My parents had permission to embellish if they wanted and make it all sound much grander than it really was. I knew that would make my mother happy.

I could just hear her on the phone with Diane. "You know she got a three picture deal for Meryl Streep and Denzel Washington. Oh yes, doing quite well. The girls? You know Jessica is an actress, and the younger one, Dana, is going to school with the Handie twins."

She wasn't a liar as such, just an embellisher. She left out parts that didn't fit the picture she was trying to paint. She added parts that painted it more beautifully.

I could hear the gossip 3,000 miles away. One of their own out in Hollywood and doing three picture deals, no less. And I was the one that they thought would be a loser because I had the baby and didn't get that degree.

For the first year or so, time just flew by. I was so focused on making my life work that I put off that call to Harris, again. It occurred to me that during the wait, he might find someone else and get married and have children. But I just held on, gritted my teeth and still didn't give another man the time of day. Dana didn't act or go on auditions. I secretly thought the only reason she even agreed to get headshots taken was because of Jessica. Jessie got a couple of small parts, but both she and I were disappointed she didn't do more.

I was making my bread and butter on the other kids I had picked up along the way. The little Salvadorian boy did a commercial first time out. It became so popular people were quoting it everywhere I went. I must have heard those lines at least 10,000 times, including on the *Tonight Show*. I started to believe I had a knack for picking winners.

The little girl with the booming voice got a soap opera and that turned out to be her big break. In fact, every little Susie and Manuel I took on did reasonably well.

I, on the other hand, completely led a double life. In the daytime, I was agent extraordinaire. Wonder woman of Hollywood child procurement. At night, I was still paying the bills by working for *Crime Calls* and I was growing more tired and more miserable by the day.

Nobody at work could understand why I was still doing the 10 PM to 6 AM shift while working for Carla Barter.

"You should just relax, woman," said one of my co-workers. "I've been here since they opened these doors and if I had the connections you have, Honey, I would be out of here in a flash." She snapped her fingers to emphasize the speed of her planned departure.

"You must be making the bucks now, just let it go and tell these people where they can stick it."

I'm sure to the outsider it probably looked like I was swimming in dough. I had started to acquire the accouterments of a real agent. No more Bug. That happened when I was told it didn't look professional enough and I should have a more 'acceptable' car. So with the residuals, commissions and a bank loan, I purchased a shiny 318i BMW dark silver/gray. In perfect condition.

The car was five years old. It just looked new. The beauty of that model was that BMW stayed with the same design for years.

I was in debt up to Mt. Everest and those clients who were making 50,000 and 35,000 per commercial were paying me only 10 percent.

Oops, I mean 5 percent. Carla was taking her 5 percent off the top. No matter what it looked like on the outside, the inside wasn't quite as pretty. I would get a check here and there for a couple thousand, but that was less often than more, and just when I thought our money worries were over, I did a little thing like getting the better car. I knew disaster was looming and before too long, I was over my head, drowning in the Southern California desert.

Chapter 31

Maybe it's just the nature of life that when one bad thing happens, others line up to spell CATASTROPHE.

The day my car overheated and the mechanic told me it would cost $675.00 to fix because it was a BMW, was the same day I broke a toe when I banged into a cement step barefoot.

It was also the same day that I found out Rose had another relapse.

Lance got a phone rigged up somehow so that I could talk to her from her hospital bed. I tried to picture Rose waif-like and weak, cloaked in hospital white. Or worse yet, some dowdy print job that she would have abhorred if she had her senses about her.

Hospital conversations always revolve around how one is feeling and naturally so, but I knew better than to ask too many questions about her health. So I talked about things we did when we were together. I asked her about food and who she had spoken to besides me. Most of her answers were quick, only a "Yes" or "No" or "Okay," and once in a while, she would get out a sentence or two. I thought maybe she didn't understand most of our conversation anyway, so I quit asking questions. I told her over and over again that I loved her and that I was praying for her to get well.

The weakness of her voice made it obvious to me she wasn't getting better. She coughed and her breathing was labored from trying to push the words out. I must have misunderstood her at one point, for in a moment of what sounded like clarity, I thought I heard her talk about coming back to the states. The phrase she uttered made me think she was dreaming of returning. We had said it to each other many times when we were in the Philippines. Talking about our lives once we went back to the states. Although the words were garbled and soft, I could hear her clearly enough to understand.

"I'll see you on the other side," she said.

Lance took the phone.

"She's tired, Leah."

"I understand. Tell her I love her and to get some rest."

A week later, he called and told me that

Rose had died at 12:15 PM that Saturday, my time. It was in April and the air was crisp in Los Angeles. The Santa Ana winds were blowing and all traces of the yellowish-brown smog had been cleared out of the valley. The sky was a glorious blue outside when I got the call.

I've replayed that moment many times. It haunts me when the night is pitch black and I am alone with thoughts of my own mortality. I was ironing. Something I never do. When the phone rang I was irritated. I didn't want to answer it. But I picked it up to hear Lance calling me from what sounded like the bottom of the ocean. I waited for him to say what I already knew. He tried to be gentle with the news. So he took a good minute to get it out.

"Leah?"

I could feel the flutter of panic rising in my chest.

"Lance, what is it?"

"Leah, Rose is gone."

There was a period of silence on both ends and then I watched in slow motion as the iron slipped from my fingers past the ironing board and hit the carpet.

I said some other words to Lance. I may have said, "I'm sorry," but I don't think so. I think it was, "Thank you," which doesn't make any sense, either. Then I hung up the phone.

The iron was burning a spot in the rug that smelled of plastic and I rushed to pick it off the floor. I cursed because I knew it had ruined the stupid carpet and I might not get my deposit back.

Chapter 32

My mind raced back to Mr. Brown telling me life wasn't fair, and I don't know why, but even him telling me that seemed unfair. You know, you do something good for someone and you get appreciated. You work towards your dreams and they come true. But I was learning that he had been right all along. Bad people sometimes get more. Good people don't necessarily find true love, or peace or health. They have money problems, and car problems, and family problems, and then sometimes they just die.

My grandfather had died when I was 13, but he was old. So I knew what to do with that. He had lived his life the way he wanted to live it, and he had some success. He had children and grandchildren and he'd finished his job on Earth. Now, that was fair.

But Rose, no. She was the one friend who didn't just disappear because we had moved away from each other. She was my strength when I was alone in the PI without anyone to call on. She was my Puerto Rican sister. The one with a NYC accent. And, she had just found her happiness.

I hated myself for the anger, but I was angry. Why was she allowed to have that dream of true love for such a short time and then have it snatched away? I began to think about death and what is it like to die. No one wants to talk about that. What had it felt like in the end? Was she scared? Was she remorseful? Did she regret some of the things that she had done in this life? Some of them put her on her deathbed. Some of them outright killed her. I knew it and so did she.

Yes, we all get the death sentence in the end. Every last one of us. But not at thirty-two.

I wondered if I was selfish to want her back.

With my photos and a box made of teak that she gave me on my 30th birthday, I crushed rose petals and prayed for her soul. I had a rosary that I found on a Greyhound bus years ago, and I put it in the box with the flowers. For a solid month, that altar remained on my dresser and I shed tears each time I glanced in its direction. Then one day, I just walked up to the dresser, removed the photos, threw them in a drawer, dismantled the altar and cried until my contacts blurred.

It seemed everyone was destined to leave.

Between Rose and Harris, I was branded. I couldn't think of, or look at another man. I should have been out dating, meeting people who might be potential mates, testing the uncharted waters, but all I could do was compare every male with Harris. None came close.

The rainy days were horrid. Maybe they reminded me too much of my life at Clark. The musty smell of the pavement and the feeling of freshness after the rain stopped. On one of those days I sat in my room praying for the LA River to flood so that the electricity would go out, and we would have to dig around for candles to light so we would be able to see in the dark. I've always been funny that way. Wanting a catastrophe. Waiting for the sky to fall. Hoping it would hurry.

My mind flashed back. Harris. The two of us clinging to each other in the rain and I would call out to him psychically, begging him to come back. It was a day like that, the clouds too full. I watched as they opened with fury. I came from working at the agency and decided enough time had passed.

My hands shook as I picked up the little note I left between the pages of *The Autobiography of A Yogi*. I could feel dozens of nasty butterflies churning in my stomach. Was this the right thing to do? Was this the right time to do it? Was he going to forgive me for what I had done?

I dialed the first number and a man about eighty years old answered to the name of Colin Harrison.

On the second try, I reached Harris's brother.

"Hello? Is this Colin?"

"Yes, it is," he answered.

"Do you have a brother named Michael?"

"Yes. Why? Who is this?"

"I don't mean to bother you, Colin but, I know, I knew, your brother. We were in the Philippines together and I have been thinking…well…wondering if you could give me his number. I would really like to contact him."

"What did you say your name was?"

"Leah, Leah Holden."

"Oh yes, Leah. Hang on." Did I sense recognition in his voice? My hands, still trembling, I scribbled the number on the side of the phonebook. I had taken the first step.

Nights were the worst. My living room/bedroom got lonelier as time went on. The puka shell lamp that hung from the ceiling reminded me. The paintings of Pangsanhang Falls reminded me. I looked around realizing I had picked up my Filipino living room and set it down intact in a Studio City apartment. The only piece of new furniture was my futon. Everything else was imported from a happier time and a more tragic one.

Over and over like a bad recording, I'd play in my mind what I had done and not done with my life. What I needed to do next. Was I in the right job? Would I even be able to make a living at it? Was I a fool for wanting it all? Was I a fool for thinking I could have Harris back again?

I have always done my best thinking in the darkest hours. It's why I've never slept well. The night comes and with it the quiet. All day the sounds and noise and brainwaves from the millions of people that inhabit this ball in space encroach on my own thoughts. They interfere with my mental process, so I am a walking zombie. Taking Dana to school, going to work, talking to clients, greeting neighbors, making dinner. But when the rest of our side of the world sleeps, then those few of us left awake have the intelligence of the universe at our command. Unfiltered by the noise.

Sometimes, in the midst of a night, a spark of brilliance emerges or an inspiration so pure that I know I must act. Other times, it is an endless road of darkness that sends me spiraling back to longing and days gone by. And always more questions than answers.

About once a month, I would repeat a little

ritual. It would start with a bit of madness. The need to rehash the years on Clark in gruesome detail. The insistence that nothing would end my despair until I was reunited with Harris. To garner up courage, I paced the floor. Hours on end until I had an almost uncontrollable desire to pick up the phone. My insides quivered from want and I knew if I could just talk to him, it would relieve my pain. I needed to tell him about Rose and my divorce. I needed to say that I still loved him. But each time I put my hand on the receiver, I felt a sickness in my head that made me stop in mid-dial. It proved my weakness. I was possessed.

I considered calling his brother once more to see if he had mentioned my call. But feeling it to be an act of desperation, thank God, I abandoned such thoughts. I was more scared of Harris's rejection than of anything I had to go through on my own. I feared he wouldn't want to hear my voice. Or worse, be repulsed by it or by my cowardice. I got nauseous. As if I ate a bad meal. As if I had been poisoned.

Once, I remember Harris and I talked about our fate. He said love comes first and providence takes care of the rest. I suspected providence was not my friend. No one waits forever. No one remains alone forever, save me. I had made my decision. Or was it providence that made it for me? The day I met Harris in his blue shirt with the sleeve rolled up. I knew then, as much as I knew anything ever, there would never be anyone else. This is why I trembled at the possibilities. If he rejected my outstretched hand, then he would destine me to a life without love. It would have been the ultimate act of faith to dial his number. I was not yet brave enough. I was not ready.

Chapter 33

Jolted awake out of a dead sleep, at first I had no idea what was happening, but when the TV on the shelf crashed to the ground, and I found myself unable to balance, I yelled to the kids.

"Earthquake. Earthquake. Get under the bed."

I could hear screaming coming from their room, so I crawled through the hallway to get to them.

"Get under the bed.," I kept yelling.

Dishes and books fell around me. The three of us climbed underneath and huddled together while the bed above us rocked for over a minute.

The news actually said it lasted 40 seconds, but I promise you, it was the longest forty seconds of my life.

"Please make it stop. God, please. Make it stop. Make it stop.," I prayed.

Transformers popped in the distance, and

with them out went the lights. With no hum of electricity to numb us to the sounds outside, every squeal and cry was amplified.

They always tell you to have flashlights, water, cash and food ready for earthquakes when you live in LA, but no one ever seriously takes that advice. I know I didn't. I had candles, but I remember somewhere hearing that you shouldn't light candles because of the gas leaks.

It was 4:03 in the morning, and now all we could see was the glare of fires on the hillsides behind our apartment complex. As the rumbling died down, a sickening smell started to seep into the bedroom. I knew there was gas leaking somewhere together with an acidy scent from spilled chemicals.

The combination couldn't be good. I didn't know if my car was buried under rubble or if I could use it. Since we lived on the second floor, if the steps were damaged how would we get down? As I looked around the floor, I could see pieces of cut glass glistening orange from the reflection of the fires. I knew we had to leave.

When Dana emerged from under the bed, I saw she was clutching a water bottle and two candy bars. She held them tight against her chest and whispered, "I told you, 'just in case.'"

I felt around for Dana's shoes. Jessie had already found hers, mine and an umbrella that she said would protect us if there were aftershocks.

"Dana. Here," I said, "put these on." I handed her the first things I could feel that would cover her feet.

"They don't match.," she yelled.

"I don't care if they match, Dana. Put the shoes on so we can get out of here."

"But Mommy, they don't match.."

We weren't going to fight over fashion in the middle of a major earthquake, so I grabbed the shoes, stuck them on her feet, threw a blanket over her and we edged our way to the front door. I was praying that the aftershock, which I knew was imminent, would hold off long enough for us to make it down the stairs.

With leaking gas and cars parked under the building, I was seriously afraid the next one would start an inferno.

We crept down the stairs ever so gingerly...looking like that family in *The Birds* when they tried to make it from the house to the car without being torn apart by crows gone mad. I saw myself playing out the movie, and as time was lagging behind me, the ground began to quiver and our descent turned into a full-fledged bolt for the car.

In our car park, the Beemer was sitting quietly, awaiting our arrival. Not a scratch on her. Not even a fallen brick. I nodded at several of the tenants on the way down. Many of them looking dazed and spinning in place. I wanted to help them, but self-preservation won out.

I passed our landlord, Sylvia, who was calling her husband, Clyde, a giant of a man. Big enough to make the sky in Montana seem small. Everyone else was screaming for him.

"Clyde you stupid idiot, get your ass out here and show us where the gas is before this whole place goes up," yelled one of the guys from a top floor window. "I swear to God, I'm going to come in there and kill you myself, if you don't."

But maybe they were all thinking what I was thinking. If he didn't hurry up, an explosion might do the job first. Sylvia was crying like a baby while the old man in 104 was running around with a big gash on his head from the bookcase that hit him. And I just wanted to get the hell out of there before something really bad happened.

I pushed Dana into the car and Jessie took the seat beside me. I heard someone say Clyde was in the dining room hiding under the table and he had vowed not to come out until the fire department showed up.

The girls and I caught one of those laugh attacks that makes you sick at your stomach, and causes tears to run down your face. Our cheeks were still tight with laughter as we passed the broken buildings and downed power lines on Ventura Blvd.

We needed water, food and a place to stay. The 7-Eleven at the corner of Magnolia and Fulton was the only place open for business. Ketchup had spilled all over the floor, and half the stock was knocked to the ground, but it was open. I pulled up and told Jessie and Dana to wait while I gathered supplies. Three bottles of water, some moon pies, a huge bag of chips, some batteries, and a plastic flashlight. There were five people waiting in line ahead of me.

I handed the guy my debit card and found out my mistake.

"Are you kidding me, lady?"

"What?"

I was trying to figure out what the problem was.

"You can't use your card, there's no power." He surveyed the place with his eyes as if to emphasize my idiocy.

"Oh, wow, yeah...I hadn't thought about that. Sorry." I just thanked my lucky stars that I at least had gas in the car, a condition that wasn't necessarily normal.

"Okay guys, it looks like we are going to hit the road," I announced when I returned to the driver's seat.

"You didn't get us anything," noticed Dana.

"Yeah, there's no power...we have to get

out of LA, far enough away so that I can use the ATM machine. I don't have cash on me."

"Great," complained Jessie. "That figures."

"It's not like I planned for an earthquake tonight, Jessica."

"You never plan anything."

So this, too, was going to be my fault.

Chapter 34

I was trying to get some news on the radio to see which directions were blocked. Fires had broken out in all areas so I had no idea which way was safe. Finally, a report came on saying that the most damage had occurred in the west side of the valley. Looked like we would be heading back out to our old stomping ground. Riverside County. They had beds and ATM machines.

"Let's go to the Holiday Inn," said Jessie.

"Why?" I asked her.

"Because it's next door to the mall," she said.

Teenagers.

I really didn't care where we went, I just wanted to get to a place where I could rest and turn on a TV.

"You come from Studio City?" asked the guy at the front desk of the Holiday Inn as he looked at my driver's license. "Must have been a pretty bad shake huh?" The TV set behind him was tuned to KBLA 6 and it was minute-by-minute coverage of the quake.

"Yeah, did they say how big it was?" I asked him.

"Talking about a 6.7 or somewheres around there. Tore up the 118 and killed a bunch of folks in an apartment someplace, too. Yep, it was a bad one."

"Did you feel it?" Dana asked him.

"Sure did, young lady…felt it good and strong. Shook all the books off the top shelf over there."

"Geez." Dana looked amazed.

I was wondering if she had forgotten that we barely escaped in the dark with things crashing down around us. She seemed more impressed with his four books on the floor than she was with all the debris we had to climb through to get out of the apartment.

Then David Shane from Channel 6 news looked up, startled, and began to dive under his desk. He stopped midway, tried to regain his composure and he sat back down in his seat.

"Christie, are you okay?" He turned to Christie Lemming his co-anchor. "Folks, it appears that we have just had a rather significant aftershock. That was quite a jolt. I'm no expert, but I would put that at about a 5.5…what do you think, Christie?"

"Yes, David, that's about right. It was a strong and jolting shake, which felt as if it might be centered very close to the studio. We will check with the USGA, and as soon as we get information on the magnitude of the latest shaker, which appeared to be an aftershock of the 4:03AM quake, we will bring it to you live, of course, on KBLA Channel 6, the Voice of the Valley."

The shaking took a few seconds to reach us. The chandelier above started to sway and the glasses tinkled. In Riverside, it was less a jolt and more of a rolling motion.

Dana had had enough shaking for one morning and she was ready to run for the door.

"Dana sit down." yelled Jessie. "It's too far away to be dangerous."

But Jessie wasn't doing much to ease her sister's fears.

"It'll do that for a while," I said. "Maybe we'll get a few big ones, too, but they aren't going to hurt you, the biggest one is over. The ground just has to get settled now. Don't worry, okay?"

Dana said, "Okay." But the wide eyes told me she wasn't a believer.

Next day, with money in hand and a good night's sleep behind us, it was time to go back and face our future. Funny, we were less than a hundred miles from LA, but the difference was staggering.

As we neared the valley, cars on the freeway thinned out. It was definitely not business as usual, and we had no idea of what we would really find once we took the off ramp towards home.

I wasn't ready to deal with what we had left behind in the apartment, so instead I headed down Moorpark to see if Carla's agency had made it through the temblor.

"Oh my God, Mom, look." Jessie couldn't believe what she was seeing and neither could I.

Buildings that two days ago had people living in them were now standing with their guts spread open.

"Jesus Christ, wonder what happened to the person in that bed," I said as we passed an apartment whose outer wall had crumbled. A bed hung over the edge of what used to be the floor. It looked as if someone had been sleeping in it when the quake hit.

"Mom. Look.," cried Jessie. She saw it before I did, and Dana saw it next.

"Oh, no." I whispered, "No…."

"Mommy? What are you going to do?" asked Dana.

I didn't know what I was going to do, or what we were going to do, or what Carla would do about the building, but from what I saw, there wasn't much left to do anything with. I started going over the possibilities in my head. She would find another location, open again, rebuild on that site. After all, it was her property.

Then I thought of something more sobering. What if that quake had happened at 4:03 PM, instead. We would have all been in that building. Me and the girls and Carla and the kids on audition, the graphic artists that rented the upstairs, and anyone else who might have been unlucky that day.

I took Ventura Blvd back to the apartment. It was as bad as Moorpark. There was still smoke trailing out of a restaurant, and most of the display windows along the road had been smashed. The street was littered with clothes, linens, appliances, and of course, broken glass and power lines. I didn't like the idea of driving around downed power lines but I figured it must be safe since there was nothing to warn us differently.

As we turned the corner, I caught a glimpse of the apartment. I had almost convinced myself it wouldn't be there. I figured the gas leak had blown it up. But there it was and it looked no worse than it usually did. You would never have known a 6.7 earthquake had visited our building the night before.

The only casualty was the staircase. The railing wobbled a bit as we climbed. And then we opened the door.

Considering the state of the building, I had not expected such a mess. I knew there would be damage. I heard it happen, but it was far worse than I had imagined.

The refrigerator had turned over on its side. Milk, ketchup, juice, eggs, and leftovers had made a mushy soup that clung to the sides of the kitchen tiles.

Every single dish, plate, and glass was now broken. The TV sat on the floor face down. When I picked it up to get a damage estimate, it looked as if Elvis had used it for target practice. Nothing that could move was left untouched. Stuff that wasn't supposed to move had been rearranged, too.

Windows broken. Door off hinges. Pipes in the bathroom hanging without the sink attached. There was no electricity. No water.

"What are we going to do?" asked Jessie. "We can't stay here."

"Yeah," I said. "We'll figure something out." But silently, I *was* figuring and it wasn't going to be easy. I was sure I only had enough left in the bank and on my credit card to get us through the next few days.

We could barely salvage our clothes. Dana insisted on taking Oscar the stuffed animal that had been on the boat with her when we went to Grande Island. I couldn't hold back the tears.

There was no victory in where I was. I had only come this far to fall behind, again. This never-ending saga of Leah and no-money-no-life-no-hope-to-fix-it that I always found myself in was getting old. Maybe I should have stayed with Mike, at least he made sure we had a roof over our heads, and, until the whole thing with Harris, he had never hit me.

Green garbage bags full of clothes and toys filled the Beemer until the backseat was so stuffed it reached the top of the front headrest. I was tired.

If I spent all of my money on hotels like Holiday Inn, we would be penniless in a week. But I couldn't live on the streets with the girls, so if that was my only option, we were better staying in the apartment and waiting for it to be repaired.

We looked at all the burned out, quaked out, ruins. We drove the area of the epicenter and spent a lot of time saying, "Oh, my God" and, "Geez," as we went. I wished I'd had a video camera or even a 35mm because this would be something to look back on when the dust settled.

Of course, all that did was bring to mind the fact that Mike had taken both of those in the divorce settlement. I was the only woman that I'd ever known who lost almost everything in a divorce. Most the time, you hear the man saying how he was taken to the cleaners. How the wife left him broke and how he had to work two jobs just to support himself and pay the alimony. I chuckled. Alimony? What's that?

My child support check couldn't even pay a month of groceries.

"Girls, listen. We have to go home," I said while pulling into a Safeway parking lot. "I'm going in to get some cleaner and more garbage bags, and some batteries for the flashlights. But we don't have a choice. There's no place else to go."

"Why don't we go back to the hotel?," asked Dana.

"Because Mom doesn't have enough money." Jessie answered with her beautiful teenaged sarcasm intact.

It seemed lately Jessica took every opportunity to show her disapproval. Never mind that I had started the whole Hollywood thing for her. I guess looking at it from her perspective, I was a horrible failure as a mother. I guess from my perspective, I was, too. I just didn't want to be reminded every time I turned around how my life was a meaningless tribute to mediocrity.

I was trying. Trying to give Jessica the career she said she wanted and trying to do something for me and Dana at the same time. It just seemed like I was cursed. Or jinxed. Or maybe born under a bad star.

Things always seemed to start off good for me, and then get complicated and fizzle in the end. Like Hollywood. Sure, I started because of Jessie, but I really liked it. So far, it just hadn't been as profitable as I had imagined.

I couldn't raise kids on talent agency money. I couldn't count on a paycheck regularly without working all night at *Crime Calls*. I had nothing in the bank worth talking about and no way to save. The beautiful slate grey Beemer was only a façade. Like those buildings on the studio lot. Lots of flash on the outside. But take a look behind them and what do you get? Nothing really solid holding them up.

As I mourned what was left of our Hollywood dream, I knew I needed help. A plan and some help. But asking meant risking humiliation, again. We didn't even have a phone that worked anymore. Who was I supposed to call? Mike was out of the question. He didn't care if I lived or died, and if I did call him he would certainly use it against me to get custody of the girls.

"See? She is an unfit mother, unable to support and care for the girls."

Never mind that his contribution made me laugh and cry in the same breath.

I could call my sister, but I was too proud.

Yes, she was younger, but I had to admit, she had done a much better job of sorting out this business called life.

Friends? I didn't really have any. Not at that level. Not the 'Hey I need to borrow some money, and by the way we need a place to live for awhile' kind. I had only stayed in one place long enough to make any real friends, and that was the Philippines.

I thought of Rose. I could have called her in a minute. She would have given up her bed for us.

Harris? I guess there was no point even entertaining that thought.

It was amazing even to me that I could end up like this. So many false starts. So many complications. Always in need. What was wrong with me?

"Jessie," I said as I picked up the car keys, "I'm going to the corner to use the phone."

I dialed and listened to it ring.

I always hated these calls. Since I left the Philippines I had kept it to good news once in a long while, like my job at Carla's, or just a Happy Mother's Day, Merry Christmas type of thing.

"Mother?"

I hesitated and then I heard her cry.

"Leah." she shouted. "*Oh, thank God*. Is everyone alright?"

"Yeah, yeah we're all fine."

"Oh, thank God. Pete. Pete. Come and get the phone. It's Leah...they're okay."

I heard my father pick up the other phone. "Leah, your mother has been so worried."

I recognized the sternness in his voice. How many times in my life had I heard that my mother was so worried? But I understood their fear, now.

"Mother, Dad..." I didn't know how to start. "I need some help."

"Of course you do," said my mother. "What about your apartment? Is it okay?"

"Not really. Everything is in ruins."

"What about the agency?" she asked.

"It's gone." That was nearly the truth.

My father interrupted. "You and those girls need to come on back home. This is foolish. There is no reason for you to be out there all alone like this. You don't know anyone and you have nowhere to go."

"I have my job at *Crime Calls* and besides, I like it here." I answered. "I know Carla...she'll rebuild the agency as soon as she can...and I can find another place to live if I have to. It's just that I don't have enough money right now, with everything that has been going on...."

"We are not going to send you money so that you can just go on like this," said my father. "You have two girls to think about and the way you are living makes no sense."

"If you want help that is fine, but you need to bring the children home." My mother added.

Bring the children home. I thought this was my home. I had a job, actually two jobs until yesterday, and so okay, I wasn't raking in the cash and I was pretending to live like a movie mogul when I still needed food stamps. But I was doing something for myself and I was doing it by myself. I had to be proud of that fact, because it was the first time I had ever really tried to make it on my own.

Now they want me to go back to Ohio, start from zero. Face the sneers of my mom's snotty friends who thought their kids had done so much more with their lives than me. I could do anything; wash walls, clean toilets, type eight hours a day, or deliver newspapers. I could do anything, but I couldn't do that.

The days of our lives seem to usually just go by in a blur. Then there are the days that change everything. I remember a few of them. The day I arrived in the Philippines. The day I met Harris. The day I decided to make it on my own. And then there was this day.

I was standing at the phone booth with the receiver in my hand when the tears started. Then the sounds that I make when I can't go on came. For over an hour I sat in the car and let them bellow out of me. Whaling over the shards and pieces of a life that shot through my brain. Pieces that when strung together found me crying at the corner of Vineland and Ventura, in a car that was too expensive, with no way to support two kids, except a stupid job at a stupid call in TV show.

When I composed myself enough, I returned to my little apartment to find the girls deep in trash removal and renovation. They gleamed with pride when I opened the front door.

"Mommy, look." Dana greeted me with a broom and dustpan. "It's getting better."

"It sure is," I said between sobs. "It's much better."

Clyde recovered from his fear long enough to board the windows and tape down the wiggly pipes. As I looked around, I had to admit that our little one bedroom, worst building in the best neighborhood apartment had survived the 6.7 quite nicely. It actually was habitable.

That night, I spread my blankets in the middle of the floor in the girls' room. Glass and rubbish had been removed and only bits of plaster from the walls gave away the disaster. Their room looked almost normal. We would use the bedroom as our safe haven, so we put shoes out beside the beds in pairs, and placed a flashlight between them. All of us were a little jumpy about a recurrence of an earthquake, but the radio had said that as the days went by, chances were slimmer. At least now we were prepared. And just like on the TV show, *The Waltons,* we had all worked hard that day and were ready for rest.

"Goodnight Mom," said Dana.

"Night Dana, night Jessie," I whispered.

"Night Mom, Night Dana, Night John Boy." giggled Jessica.

Maybe we would be okay after all.

Chapter 35

"Carla? Have you seen it?" I called her early the next morning.

"Yes, Siree, sure did. It's a fright. Boy, that one really tore things up, didn't it?" She almost sounded cheerful.

"What are you going to do?" I asked.

"Hell, girly, where I come from there's always something a poppin'. Why, we've got twisters and floods that'll knock you clear from here to Topeka. And now and again, we even get a hurricane or two down by the Gulf. Hell, any a'them does more damage than that little ole thing did. Now just leave me a minute to think over it. I'll come up with a plan in a couple a days. Don't you worry your little head over this thing. We'll be up and running again before you can get yourself a good night's sleep."

I was trying to muster the kind of optimism that Carla had, but from my vantage point, it would be months before I would be able to go back to work for the agency. I had a thought in that moment of leaving Carla to go to a bigger and better talent agency. I didn't have the luxury of waiting around for her to rebuild an entire structure. I needed to make money. And my clients needed to work. I had so few of them that every job meant rent or gas for me.

"Just relax, girly. Take your kids out for an ice cream and give me a minute. You know the show must go on. So don't you fret."

I was happy to give her that minute, but I was worried her minute might be a long one. Nevertheless, I was in a no-win situation for the time being. Nobody was going to hire me three days after the largest earthquake to hit the LA area in 40 years, and I was in no position to be running around amidst the debris trying to go on interviews if they were.

At least my job at *Crime Calls* was safe, although we still had to shut down for a week because of the electrical problems. I was so happy I hadn't taken the advice of my well-meaning co-workers who thought I had made it in Hollywood and could do without that job.

Dana was having trouble sleeping. I was, too. I could feel every inch of movement whether it came from the ground or the guy next door cleaning his apartment. Hyper-vigilance. Every squeak and creak made me jump.

We had no power for three more days, so it was probably good that all work was canceled. I wouldn't have wanted to leave the girls alone after the trauma of a major earthquake just under our belts.

My mind wanted a way out. I looked for a fix-all but couldn't think of any. Then, I stooped to the place I hadn't wanted to go.

After one of our sight-seeing trips, we stopped off at Griffith Park. We weren't alone. The park's occupancy had climbed with the advent of the quake. Along the winding road that led to the LA Zoo there must have been a thousand parked cars. Blankets dotting the greenery like an abstract painting, and some people were even equipped with tents and sleeping bags. After what we had all been through, I couldn't blame them. One family sat in their lawn chairs gathered around a portable television. I felt like a voyeur peeking inside their living room.

We only had what we had carried out the morning of the quake. Garbage bags were still stuffed in the Beemer, since I was afraid of hauling them back up the stairs, not sure if another shaker would send us running out in the night. We salvaged Dana's bedspread from the backseat and settled down for our meal.

"How would you guys feel about going

back to Ohio?" I asked.

Dana immediately jumped up and down. "You mean to see Mama and Daddy Pete?"

"Well yes, I mean that, but I mean to stay."

"No way." Jessie shouted at me. "I just got my SAG card and now you want to go and give it all up? No way. I'm not going. I'm staying. You can go."

The SAG card was a big deal. The famous union card with a 'Catch 22' attached. You can't work in reputable films or TV shows without it, and you can't get one until you get a job with one of those productions. I won't even bother with how to get around the whole problem, but she had a point. Now that she had the SAG card, her chances of working and making more money had skyrocketed. It was a bad time for her to consider moving away.

Dana only knew Mama and Daddy Pete from when she was a baby. I don't think she really remembered them except as pictures. I had done a good job of keeping my parents child rearing practices and philosophies away from the kids. Definitely from Dana, so I could understand her wanting to go live in a big house in the country. Complete with a pond and apple trees and lots of rooms to spread out. With her own bedroom again and even the Irish Setter, Buzzy, was still there. For Dana it was idyllic.

For me it was defeat. For Jessie, it wasn't even an option.

I waited for over a week to hear from Carla again. While waiting, I pondered my parents' offer. I could go, but if I did, I would be back in the same place I was before I went to the Philippines. Not just the same place, but the same state of mind and that was ultimately worse. I was divorced this time, so that part was different, but I still would have somebody else pulling my strings. I took out the book that Harris gave me and read some of it. The story was about a young man who lived in India years ago and how realized his destiny was to go to the west and teach spirituality to America.

I hadn't found my destiny yet. When I met Harris, I was sure he was a part of it. Then I left him. Rose came into my life at the same time, and so she must have been a part of it, too. But now she was gone.

I had wanted to be a nurse midwife. I was so far from that I couldn't see how it played a part anymore. It was a good idea so that I could make enough money to support myself and the girls. But my heart wasn't really in it.

On day ten, the phone rang.

"Girly, let's meet over in Burbank, at 4597 Radford tomorrow around oneish."

I had no idea where or what that was, but if Carla said to meet, I was going to meet. When I arrived, I saw the sign. The same one that had hung on the front window of the agency that was now in heaps:

THE CARLA BARTER TALENT AGENCY

The building was brick on the outside with shrubbery dotting little window boxes, which made it look oddly cozy and modern at the same time. The word, *Push,* greeted me on the glass door. That word was never on the old door. But then the old door was wooden with a knob.

The place looked like it had been built in the '70s, which would have made it about 18 years, instead of the 1930s like the other building. Not that I had anything against that old building. I kind of liked its character, but it proved they didn't do such a great job creating places that held up in major earthquakes back then.

The floors in the new place were hardwood with Persian rugs decorating the waiting area. She had invested in soft sofas and mustard-colored chairs. And movie posters graced the walls. She still had some of the black-and-white photos of her and the old-timers like Bob Hope, Lucille Ball, Elizabeth Taylor, Lawrence Welk, Glenn Ford. But they were framed and arranged in groupings above the chairs. I suspected she had hired a decorator. This looked like a Hollywood agency was supposed to look.

Then I realized something. It appeared she had started up without me.

I walked up to the front counter and had visions of the first time I met her. "Leah, come on in and let's sit yourself down."

I had never seen her in such neat surroundings. Her desk was sleek black and modern. Behind her was a wall plastered with pictures of her 80 or so clients. All working actors. Not a loser in the bunch.

I sat on one of the two black leather chairs that were also new purchases. They still had that new leather smell. I loved the smell, but hated the thought of the animal who had given its life to make the chair.

"What do you think of my little ole office now, girly?"

"It's amazing," I said, taking it all in.

"Well it's about time I moved into the 20th century, don't you think?"

I smiled.

"Look girly, I'm not gonna beat around the bush with you. I've seen what you can do. You've done a bang up job. But that ole quake was kind of a wakeup call. You know what I mean?"

I wasn't sure I did. But I agreed.

"You've got yourself a few good clients. And I give you credit. You came in here green as an apple, but you pulled it off and got you some good workers. You've made a little bit of money at it, too. But that isn't gonna get you what you need and you know it."

She was right. I needed something more. I needed a…

"A career, by golly that's what you need." Slamming the desk full force. "You can't be play-acting at this thing anymore. I know you've been doing a bit here and a bit there, but Honey you're burning the candle at both ends. Working for me and working for that show, and then trying to be a mommy, too."

I was in total agreement.

"You gotta commit girly. I mean full time. All or nothing. You need to be here and give 150%."

Never mind that I couldn't stand that phrase because in the end, 100% is all there is of anything.

"What you need to do is get yourself about 25 or 30 of those kids. Just like the ones you have now. Workers. Now if you can do that, I am telling you, you won't have to be slaving at any other job, and then girly, you will have yourself a real future."

"Yeah, you're right Carla, but…"

"Now don't 'but' me girl. I know you have money troubles and I told you I was going to give you a chance. Like I said you've shown yourself to be good at this. So here's what I'm proposing. I will give you a salary, and you know, as well as I know, that isn't done in this business, but I am gonna do it because I know if you can just get those clients, and I don't care what you have to do to get them, you will do well. Now what do you make at that *Crime Talk*?"

"*Crime Calls*." I corrected her. "About $1200.00, bring home."

"Whew." she whistled. "And you're raising kids on that? No wonder you've got yourself money problems."

I was waiting for her to say she would double it.

"Alright. Then I'll match it if you'll go out there and quit that damn job so you can put in a good day's work here."

We walked to the back offices. Then I saw the name on the door. She had counted on me more than I had counted on myself. The plaque engraved in silver tone read: Leah Conners, Children's Agent. I opened the door to see a room filled with yellow cubbies for headshots, my own breakdown machine, a computer on my desk, file cabinets, and even better, the décor was perfect for a children's area. Small chairs in primary colors, and a waiting area of my own. She pretended it was because I would look more professional that way, but she had made no secret that she really hated kids, and I was sure she figured this was the best way to keep them out of her hair.

I drove home in tears. So thankful. Yet so sad. Other than Jessie and Dana, the two people I wanted to share this with were nowhere to be found.

Somewhere in that valley I needed to come up with enough kids who could sing, dance or act to help me make a living in my newfound career. I stalked every workshop and acting school I could find. Lurking in the back of the auditoriums at school plays. Spying on families as they walked through the malls. Scoping out the prospects at the local playground.

What talent I didn't find on the street, I was sure to find if I just started calling in the folks who sent me photos. And I got pictures by the hundreds. One by one, I brought them in for interviews.

The multitudes that passed through my door staggered me. And still I couldn't find twenty-five kids who could deliver two lines with gusto.

Chapter 36

Slowly, I started acquiring the Big Twenty-five, as I called them. I found two little towhead sisters at the Farmer's Market. I was picking Fuji apples and the small one, who sounded as if she was at least 21 came up and started asking the vendor which fruit had the most Vitamins B and D. Her older sister then intervened and told the man to pay her no mind, as she had just learned about those vitamins from their mother. They had hair that hadn't been cut, maybe ever, and clothes that looked like they had been saved from the sixties, but when I saw their mother the pieces fit. She had blonde dreadlocks, a tie-dyed t-shirt, and a cotton skirt that looked imported from India. To complete the perfect image, she carried a multicolored knapsack and had a tattoo of a butterfly on her foot, which was bare like the other one.

The girls, Ocean and Pearl, started doing

commercials after very little coaching and landed a huge one together. The residuals alone kept Dana, Jessie and me in food for months.

By then, Jessie had only done a *Married with Children,* an *ER,* and a movie, which went straight to video. But she had started to gain a reputation as a decent actress. Her auditions went up and so did her callbacks, and with her SAG card in hand, I was hopeful that things would pick up for her. Then, without missing a beat, she made a one-eighty.

Late one night, as I was dozing off, she walked into my bedroom, AKA the living room. The old '40s movie *Back Street* was on and even though it was one of my favorites, the sandman was closing in. I had the volume down low so as not to disturb the girls' sleep, so I thought it was the movie when I heard a voice close by. I looked up and saw Jessie sitting on the edge of the futon.

"Mom, I need to talk to you about something important," she said. She sounded worried. I woke myself, by sitting up straight so that I could hear what was wrong. At that hour, it had to be something major.

"It's about the business."

"You mean acting?"

"Yeah…Mom…I know you put in a lot of time and hard work for me to be an actress, and I know it cost a lot of money, too…but I don't think I like it anymore."

Are you kidding me? She had gone on about 60 auditions and hadn't gotten parts like she, or I thought she would. Maybe she was just discouraged.

"It takes a while before you can really do well. Everything doesn't just work out overnight. I don't want you to give up just because you've had a few disappointments. Is it because you didn't get that part on *The Time Traveler*?"

"No Mom, I've been thinking about it a lot. I mean, of course that upset me, but that's not it. I think I want to go to college."

I had given up on the idea of Jessie attending college. She was so dead set on becoming a actress. That was the dream we were chasing.

"Remember when I was a little girl and I told you I wanted to be a veterinarian?" The mention of it took me way back to the time before Clark, before we left Ohio. She spent a summer helping out at the Myers horse farm down the road. It was in a time when I was muddy and she was clear. The mornings there were thick with dew and grass smelled clean. She would rise with the sun, off to make her way down the road, walking, or sometimes skipping until she reached the end of our driveway and entered the yard where the

Myers barn stood. She was, 'working,' she said.

Each morning, I watched her from the window on the second floor as she crossed the six acres of Mama and Daddy Pete's to get to the other side of the road. She'd turn and look back to see if she could see me peeking through the curtains. I'd open the screen and stick my hand out to wave. Then, for the next few hours she fed and brushed horses. When the colts came, she would fly into the house in a state of ecstasy, telling anyone who would listen about the birth, and all the gory bloody details about how it popped out of the mother. I had forgotten those days and how she said she wanted to be a vet back then.

"I've always wanted to be a vet. I know it now. I'm positive."

"You've changed your mind more than once, and that's okay because everybody has the right to a change of direction. You are never locked into anything. But being a vet is a big commitment. To study all the years it takes to get through college and then veterinary school. This isn't something to just decide on the spur of the moment."

"It's not the spur of the moment, Mom. I told you, I have been doing a lot of thinking."

"How long?" I asked her. "How much time have you really put into thinking about this?"

"I'll tell you the truth," she said. "But

promise not to get mad at me?"

"Go ahead," I said. Annoyance started to surface. I could hear it. Telling me not to get mad was like inviting someone to a fight. All that it said is I was supposed to get mad at the information that was about to be divulged.

"Okay…well right after we moved here and you got the job at Carla's…and I started going out on interviews...I really didn't like it. I couldn't tell you, you know we had just moved…and you gave up the job at the BX and everything to come here. So I thought you would be mad."

"Oh, Jessie." I couldn't believe what I was hearing. For a second anger roared in my brain. I saw red and was about to lash out. The move, the money, the job. All the changes I made in my life just so she could follow some notion.

She started to cry.

"Mom, I'm so sorry."

I held her against my shoulder until it was wet with tears.

Who was I to get crazy because she wanted to do something different with her life than I expected? I had done with mine what I wanted, not what my parents wanted.

"Jessie, it's not important. I don't care. I'm happy with my job. You know that. I enjoy it. And I'm good at it. And I've never been good at any job before. So I will still want to do it even if you aren't an actress. And, look," I said, trying to sooth her by rubbing her back, "it was your dream that allowed me to find mine. Don't you understand that?"

I walked to the bathroom to get her a tissue, which in my house we also called toilet paper. When I got back, she practically knocked me down, she hugged me so tight.

"Then it's okay?"

"Of course it is. You have to do what makes you happy. And as long as you do that, I'll be proud of you. As long as you don't become a bank robber or a drug dealer." I poked her in the sides. "Have you thought about when you want to start college?"

As usual, she had thought of everything. She went to her room and pulled out the catalog for Los Angeles Valley College. Big, red circles surrounded the courses she planned to take for the spring semester. She had even been to the campus counselor to find out the requirements for transferring to UC Davis when the time came because they had the best veterinary school on the West Coast. My little Jessica was growing up.

Chapter 37

Kid actors came in several varieties. There were always the ones who were so darned cute they didn't really have to do much other than just stand there and look adorable. They got famous on their looks. The Handie Twins were a good example. Being twins didn't hurt, either.

Others required more imaginative marketing. Like the quirky ones. The ones with buck teeth or neon orange hair. Freckles and big ears fell into that category as well. Unfortunately, so did those who were overweight. These kids were perfect for commercials, as they often had quirkiness hard wired into their personalities as well as their looks.

I was especially attracted to the child prodigies. Those precocious little minds that baffled their parents into wondering if they had been switched at birth. Smart kids with photographic memories made wonderful actors. They could memorize pages of dialogue and cry on cue.

But there were also the tragic ones. The poor kids who not only couldn't act or sing or dance, but knew it and didn't even want to be a part of the whole business. At the insistence of Mom or Dad (as much as I hate to say it, 'stage mother' was actually appropriate) they went obligingly to do the rounds. How many agents had seen them before me? I suspected that these kids did a bad job on purpose just so that someone would tell their parents to take them home and give up on acting.

Sometimes, that someone turned out to be me.

When I pulled out the cereal commercial script, and asked a 10-year-old to go and practice in the waiting area, I was always filled with anticipation and excitement. Because just as much as the parent wanted their child to be the next big star, I wanted it, too. I wanted it so much.

Then I would go to the waiting area and call the child into my office.

"You can come in now," I would say in a friendly voice. I would then have to tell the parent, "I'm sorry, but you will need to wait outside. We will just be a few minutes."

I never had a parent tell me that was unacceptable.

Once we were in the office, we had a little conversation. I asked a few questions to assess intelligence and the ability to think quickly, and then I would plunge on into the reading.

"Okay, you can go ahead and start anytime you want. Just do it as naturally as you can."

And out it came.

"I like Post toe-ah-sta-e-s bee- uh–cause it is buh-eh-ter then all the ooh-ther carn fluh-aa-kuh-ses. It is great."

Wonderful. And from a ten-year-old no less. Kudos to the California public schools.

At that point I'd say, "Okay sweetie, you can go outside and look at some of the games. Would you ask your parents to come in so I can talk to them?"

This is when it got really good.

So I would tell the parents, "You know in this business it is really important for a child to read well. There are many parts that require extensive memorization, and reading skills are essential. My suggestion is to have her go home and make her understand how important schoolwork is, when she has improved academically you can reconsider. But for the time being, she's not ready."

Most of the time, that was the end of it. Parents and child would pack up and go on their way. But in one case, that was only the beginning. A little boy, about eight, with the proverbial two front teeth missing, and shy as a cub, came for an interview with his father. The poor kid's reading was horrible. To be honest, it wasn't a reading at all. He never pulled his head up out of his t-shirt long enough to actually say anything. I could tell he was traumatized and I was certain he was being forced to perform.

So, I asked him, "Trevor, do you want to be on TV?"

He stared at me, then lowered his head, but said nothing.

"Do you want to be an actor?" I pushed further.

He continued to look at the floor.

"Trevor, if this isn't what you want to do, you don't have to do it. Is it your daddy's idea?"

He snapped his head up and looked me square in the eye.

"You know, not everyone wants to be on TV. Some kids would rather do other things. Like doing quiet things in their room or playing baseball. Is there something you like better than acting?"

For the first time, I got a smile.

"Painting." He said in a tiny, weak voice.

"Did you say *painting*? You mean painting pictures?"

He shook his head, hesitating before he

nodded.

"I think that is wonderful. You're an artist?"

He nodded his head again, with more enthusiasm.

"Well then, that is what you should do. You should be an artist. I'll bet you paint beautiful pictures. What kind of things do you like to paint?"

I had opened the floodgates. The next few minutes were filled with vivid descriptions of pictures he had created. Animals and kites, trees and mountains. He loved painting mountains.

"You must be a very talented painter. We all have talents, you know, but not all of us have the same ones. So it sounds to me as if art is yours."

He smiled a big, toothless grin and it was clear who pulled the strings. I sent him out to play and brought the father in to talk.

"I had a chance to spend quite a bit of time with Trevor. You know, he doesn't really belong in show business, Mr. Glover. He is very shy, and kids who really want to do this work are of an opposite temperament. "

"He's not shy," Mr. Glover said. "He's nervous. Anyone would be nervous coming to a place like this."

"Yes, I imagine that's true," I continued. "But in the entertainment industry he would be asked to perform instantly. No time to warm up or get over his initial nervousness. I'm sorry Mr. Glover, but that is the nature of the business. There is just no place for a child who is an introvert."

"You're calling my kid an *introvert*?" He glared at me. "You don't know anything about him. Look, if he messed up the lines, then give him another piece to read and I will help him this time."

"It's not a matter of messing up. He didn't even read the lines. To be honest with you, I don't think he wants to act. He told me he paints. And from the sound of it he is good at art. Why don't you encourage that talent instead? I think it would make Trevor very happy."

"Paints? Paints? Are you serious? Every kid paints."

And that was the end of the conversation. He walked out slamming the door so hard the glass on my desk shook. I followed, trying to salvage the interview and at least end on a civil note. As he passed his son sitting in the waiting area, he leaned down pointed a finger inches from the child's face, and said, "You told her you *paint?* Are you crazy? You stupid idiot."

Then he raised his hand behind him as if the next thing to happen would be a slap that could knock the kid straight into the hospital.

"Hey. Hey. Stop that." I screamed trying to position myself between Trevor and his father. "You are not going to abuse this boy in front of me. That is enough."

Mr. Glover stopped dead in his tracks as I spoke. His shocked expression told me he wasn't used to people talking to him that way.

Then he turned around and ran, I mean *ran*, out the door of the office building and down the street with Trevor still sitting on a red plastic chair. I wasn't sure what the next step was. If he came back, was I going to give the child to this lunatic? I could call child welfare, but…maybe the police. I went to get Carla.

"What the hell was that all about?," Carla asked. "Sounds like you had a riot starting down there."

Once I calmed down and explained, we thought over the options and decided the only thing to do was contact the police.

Luckily, once in a long while, the Los Angeles police respond in a reasonable amount of time. And this time, they made it fast enough to be present just as Mr. Gerald Glover arrived sweating and out of breath, to collect Trevor. He was arrested on the spot, and it turned out that there was a custody issue, so Trevor's mother was called and she picked him up within the hour.

That night was just another one when work

followed me home. Sometimes, it was the kitten I knew I couldn't keep. The one so persistent, a warm corner and bowl of milk didn't seem too bad. And other times it was the wasp that got trapped inside the car while I was driving down the 101 at 60 miles an hour. Regardless, it was always with me. Phones rang at all hours of the night for early call times in the morning. Last-minute travel arrangements had to be dealt with after the *Tonight Show* went off, and I swore like a sailor every time I turned on the television. Something would trigger my mind to remind me of an unfinished contract or workshop I had forgotten. It got so I couldn't watch a decent half hour of television or go to the movies.

I barely put my work aside long enough to get eight hours of rest, but the night of Trevor Glover, work even followed me to bed. I hated the idea of parents dragging kids around town. Forcing them to perform like trained seals. The poor things living out somebody else's fantasy of becoming a movie star. I wanted to jail all the moms and dads who behaved as if they had children for their own pursuit of money, power or happiness. Was it just an easier way to make money? Is that what they thought? Another get-rich quick scheme. Well, no matter what the motive, Coogan's Law made certain that wouldn't happen. Even if they did have the next Kirk Cameron, the new law forced parents to put the money in a trust fund.

What was my role in this drama? Was I an accomplice in prostituting children for parental satisfaction? Making puppets out of tiny bodies that should be playing instead of rehearsing lines? Was that what I had become?

I made myself a promise that night if I was going to continue representing kids not one would pass through the threshold without my first making darned sure they were doing it because they wanted to. At 2:00 in the morning, I had visions of going to nursing school and becoming a midwife, even though I knew it could never excite me the way working in Hollywood did. At five, I had images of teaching 4th grade. And the thing was, I hopped up at seven, raring to start the day.

Chapter 38

The next week, while sitting at my desk drinking what was probably my tenth cup of coffee for the day, Dana confronted me with her newfound life plan. Since Jessie had just turned her world upside down, I don't know why I was surprised at my younger one declaring she had now found her passion.

Dana had been going to the agency with me every day after school. It was easier than sending her to an after-school daycare center, but mostly, it was cheaper. And although commissions were trickling in, and I had my salary, it was still a balancing act to keep the three of us with a roof over our heads.

Dana usually sat in the kids waiting section. She set up her study area the same way each day, with books on the little yellow table while she faced the wall I had decorated with a mural of the *Wizard of Oz* characters. She faithfully did her homework and she kept up her straight A average.

But even through math and American history, she had one ear tuned to the children as they delivered their lines. By the time midyear rolled around, Dana had probably heard a hundred kids do the cereal commercial, if not more. She had watched the revolving door of parents and children and she started to display an instinct about which ones were good and which ones I would toss out in less than five minutes. Once or twice a day, she would peak in after I had auditioned a kid and she would give me her opinion on whether they had any chance at all in Hollywood. So when she popped in the office this time, I was sure she had a few choice comments about the last girl I had seen.

"Hey Mom, you know what?" She sat down in one of the two wooden parent chairs and swung her legs back and forth.

I was busy entering the last girl's information in the computer. I probably said, "Huh?" but definitely not more.

"I can do as good as she can," Dana said.

Without looking up I continued typing. "What do you mean, Hun?" I asked her.

"With that commercial. I think I can do it better than she did."

"Oh yeah?" I kept typing.

"I know you don't think I can, but I really

can, Mom. Why don't you ever give me a chance?"

I could hear how sincere she was. Maybe I hadn't taken Dana's interest in show business seriously enough. She was such a shy, quiet child. I remember when she was in kindergarten, the teacher called me to say she was worried about Dana, because she never lifted her head high enough for anyone to see her face.

I looked up and saw the fierceness in her eyes. "Okay. If you want to do the commercial, go for it."

She stood up. She began reciting the words, and as they tumbled from her lips she lit up the room. She literally glowed. It was so powerful, she gave off electricity. With magical pre-teen smile and a voice that sounded like a song, she delivered the best audition I had ever heard. My own daughter had the 'it' factor that I had been searching for in all the others. I was overcome with delicious excitement. To my amazement, my wallflower had blossomed into an amazing little actress.

"Am I good?," she asked when she finished.

"Wow. Are you *good*?" I practically screamed. "You are *amazing*."

"So now will you start sending me out on more stuff?"

It was a fair question. I had carried her as a

client. But truthfully, I never spent much effort on her career. I thought she wanted to act because of Jessica, and I didn't feel she had it in her. But she had proven to me that I had underestimated her.

"Are you telling me that you like acting now?"

"I always liked it, but you were doing all that stuff for Jessie, and I was scared 'cause I thought she was better than me."

"Well you don't have to worry about that anymore. I have never seen anyone better than you. Starting right now, Dana Holden is my number-one client. Tomorrow, we are getting you new headshots."

I was sending headshots and resumes out like a madwoman. She was getting more calls than all of my other clients put together. And to everyone's amazement, including Carla's, she nailed almost every audition. I heard reports back from casting directors. The comments went like, "This child is the best actress I have ever seen." And it wasn't because she was related to me, either. No one knew. She was a Holden and I was using my maiden name, so there was no direct connection.

I wasn't sure who this kid was anymore, or how it happened, but I guessed all the hours she spent listening to bad actors must have taught her how to be a real actress.

The highlight of the year in Hollywood is pilot season. For actors, it's better than Christmas. It's when all the new shows for the next year are cast and tested. When February and March come around, all the hopefuls from El Paso to Boston come running to Hollywood with dreams of getting a chance to interview for a spot on one of the newest TV shows. Parents give up jobs and move their offspring to the Lakeview Apartments. They sit on a hill overlooking the studios in Burbank and all the wannabees hang out at the pool in the evening, salivating over the fact that right down that hill are Warner Brothers and Disney. Those two months are Hollywood at its best and worst depending on which side of the fence you are on.

When pilot season arrived, for the first time, my clients started getting callbacks to see the producers. Three of them were on the list to be interviewed by network executives. Number one on that list was my daughter, Dana. Four of my boys, including the one from the commercial that was so big, got recurring roles on sitcoms; that meant they were guaranteed six episodes. And most of my clients were doing national commercials. One of the hippie sisters landed a supporting role in a major motion picture, and Dana got the second lead in a TV series as the daughter of the star.

Her big break was a nighttime soap opera about the family of a newly elected US president. Most of the story line revolved around his wife, who we find out has bipolar disorder and is alcoholic; and the kids, a 16-year-old boy, who it seems is an adrenaline junkie; a 12-year-old girl (Dana's character) who has an artistic temperament, wears all black and is prone to bouts of melancholy; and their youngest, a six-year-old boy with ADD. It wasn't light viewing by any means. At first, I wondered about how well the show would fare, but in a very smart marketing ploy, the network had hired the hottest teen hunk to play the older son. I knew that move alone would pull all the teenage girls who would without a doubt tune in just to drool over him. Appropriately, it was named *Family First.*

With Dana and my other clients, things started to look up. My commission of 5 percent was getting bigger. Monthly income was climbing slowly but steadily, and with all those kids working regularly, there was some sense of security in the job. I often found myself wondering why in the world the stupid Screen Actors Guild had set the ceiling for commission at a measly 10 percent. Seemed to me agents should be able to get more than that. Anyone who thought it was an easy job should spend a week from 8:00 AM 'til God knows, trying to get people hired for acting parts that at least 200 other agents are trying to fill as well. Yeah, I think they should try it.

My 10 percent had to be cut with Carla. It was just the way things worked. I thought someday it would be nice if I had the entire 10 percent for myself, but that meant opening my own agency. It was a someday thought. But there was no price on fantasizing, as I well knew. I dared to believe my luck had changed. I mouthed to myself so as not to disturb the delicate balance, "The curse has been broken."

Dana was picked up for 13 episodes (it figures, that would prove to be my lucky number). Although we weren't rich, we were far better off than we had ever been before.

You'd think that having a co-starring role in an hour series would make Dana a millionaire instantly. But it really doesn't work that way. She got a decent paycheck. More money for the 13 episodes than I ever made in a year of work. So I got my 5 percent and Carla got her 5 percent and then we used another 15 percent for Dana's career, headshots, acting coach, drivers to lessons for everything you can have a lesson on. Dana was her own little corporation, but the majority of her money had to go to the trust fund. That money had to be socked away so that when she turned 18, she wouldn't hire an attorney and sue me like half of all child actors did before the parents were required to put the money in trust funds.

It isn't easy thinking your life has turned around when all you have known is sorrow and defeat. I wanted to believe that old Mr. Brown was wrong and there was such a thing as fairness. Had life finally started to hear my cries in the night and begun rewarding me for all the years of pain and hard work?

I put in my time, got punched in the gut, shot in the heart, and I was still standing. I demanded comeuppance for those lonely years I spent with Mike, and the loss of Rose, and the heartbreak of missing Harris. If there was ever a way to make things okay after what I had been through, maybe being able to live comfortably was the payoff. I had to consider that all the troubles I'd seen were to put me on the right road.

Like Harris had said, "There is sympathy of all things." The strings that bind one person to another place and time all work together to take us on this journey and lead us in the direction of our destiny. I felt like destiny had found me more than once, and now I felt it had me doing work that I was meant to do. But nothing, not money or success, or pride in my accomplishments, or Jessie's or Dana's, took away the loss of love. It hung like a veil over my brightest victories. My heart was still vacant.

Chapter 39

Time was passing fast. It was 1990, and the door for getting back with Harris was closing around me. I was sure of it. I could feel it in my bones. If I didn't do something soon, it would be too late. I just knew he would never understand why I didn't at least make an attempt to call him. The craziest thing of all was that I wanted to so badly. I had no idea what was wrong with me. I needed him desperately.

Anyone else in my position would have been on top of the world. There were moments when I knew joy. More and more of those moments as time went by. But the undercurrent that kept me tied to Harris never stilled despite the good times. I had kept my promise to him, I had not looked at another man for over seven years.

My life was consumed with work and the girls. Friends were not a part of my vocabulary. They existed in another time. I only had acquaintances. Not girlfriends that talk about their lives and loves. When I was back at *Crime Calls,* I had made a friend, Janice. She was a phone buddy. We hardly saw each other after I left and went fulltime at the agency. But, sometimes late at night we would talk for an hour or so, and she would tell me I was a "crazy fool" for continuing to put my hopes of love on a reunion with Harris.

"Girl, you need to get over it," she'd say. "Ain't no man worth all that grief. You got to get your ass back out there on that horse."

The idea of a woman my age being celibate just irked her to the point of hysteria. She thought I was 'certifiable.' But I wasn't celibate because I had taken on the nun's habit, although I know an outsider would see it that way. It was because I wouldn't be with a man I didn't love. I loved Harris. Simple. If it wasn't him, it wasn't anybody.

"If you don't call him, then how are you ever going to get this over with?" she asked one night.

I had to deal with my fear. Why couldn't I just pick up the damn phone and make the call? What was the worst that could happen?

I made a mental note to do it before the end of the week.

While I shuffled paper and phone calls, Dana had to be on the set most of the time.

When she got home, she still had no down time. No time to watch *The Simpsons* or *Saved by the Bell* because she had so many lines to memorize each night.

The lives of a Hollywood talent agent and a child actress work like this: At home by eight and up at daybreak. We never went anywhere except the studio, my office, and to pick up miscellaneous items for the business. Jessica bought a little red hatchback that she drove to Valley College so there was no need to chauffer her anymore.

When the weekend came, we had to get in all the shopping and errands that were stuck on hold while everything else we did revolved around show business. Saturday mornings we reserved for grocery shopping. And it was at the Ralph's on Ventura Blvd and Laurel Canyon, the day after *Family First* aired the pilot episode that it happened. We were going down the aisle of baked goods. Dana was telling me about one of the women on the set who did the makeup and how 'cool' she was. I heard whispering and then all of a sudden I noticed we were being followed. Three typical valley girls, dressed in mini-skirts and tank tops were less than 10 paces behind us everywhere we went. They were giggling and staring and I had had just about enough.

I turned about to find out what they

wanted. It was going to be a stare down. After a weeklong emotional rollercoaster and PMS to boot, they were messing with the wrong woman. The three of them moved in, walking right past me and up to Dana who looked like she needed an invisible shield to keep them out of her personal space. She backed into the cookie stand.

"Aren't you that girl on *Family First*?"

Dana did a great imitation of a trapped animal. I think she was eyeing an opening so that she could make a run for it. She may have been comfortable in front of the camera, but she definitely inherited a recluse gene, and she seemed bewildered by the attention.

When she nodded yes, one of them practically jumped in the air. "See. I told you that was her." Another one told her that she "loved the show."

Then they bopped off from whence they came.

Both of our eyebrows flew up a couple of inches. We couldn't believe it.

"You're a star, kiddo."

"Wow, looks that way, huh?," she said.

That was just the beginning. Our entire existence seemed to reinvent itself overnight. Just going to the gas station or the grocery store with Dana became a chore at times. People outside Hollywood think it is so dad-blasted glamorous being on TV. But they don't see the times when you stay at home instead of dealing with the looky loos who just want to gawk or get an autograph. We were still living in the worst-building-best-street in Studio City, but when Dana got her 15 minutes, I found out with fame came expectations and we couldn't stay in our little one bedroom any longer because word had gotten out that Dana Holden lived there.

I was proud of her success. Jessie was proud of her, too but all the attention was making her life harder as well.

"See, Mom," Jessica said to me, "this is what I would have had to deal with if I kept working. It's not worth it."

We all kind of have a bit of the hermit crab in our DNA. I've always said it was the Native American part that did us in. We have always been quiet. All three of us. Jessie less so, I guess. More like her dad. Not that we couldn't project when we wanted to, mostly we just didn't want to. And the type of interference that Dana's show was having on our peaceful lives was a pain, even if it was a welcome one.

When Hollywood forces you to play by its rules, you have to play. We moved to the security building a month after *Family First* got extended for 13 more episodes. The ratings were climbing and it looked like the show was going to run for at least another year or two. I was in the process of re-negotiating Dana's contract since she had fulfilled the first 13. She could demand a bigger salary and that was money in my pocket, so I was fairly certain we would be able to pay the rent for the duration of our lease.

The Academy Village was where all the up and coming actors and singers lived. It sat five stories high on a one-block area. Painted pale pink stucco on the outside. The southwestern theme had taken over, and all the new buildings were desert beige or pink. The best thing though, was that it had underground parking and a security guard on duty 24 hours a day. The front door was bulletproof glass, which was a necessity because the memory of Rebecca Shaefer being murdered on her doorstep was still fresh in the minds of all of us.

Nobody was doing anything in that building without someone seeing it. There were cameras in the elevator, the parking structure, the stairwells, hallways and I was praying that was all. I had moments when I would cover my breasts in my own bathroom, paranoid that Big Brother had invaded the inner sanctum.

Life was moving so fast that I couldn't keep up with the string of changes. Money was no longer the first thing on my mind in the morning and the second to the last thing when I went to bed. Of course, the last thing was still always Harris. I knew I had done what I set out to do. I was making a living and I had created a life that I loved. Nobody could take the joy of that away from me. I didn't need Mike or my parents, or my sister or anyone to support me any longer. I didn't need a life with Harris because I was desperate. I wanted a life with him because I still loved him more than I loved almost anything else. I had put off the inevitable long enough and I wanted to share my success with the one person who I knew would be happy my life had turned out this way.

Again I wanted to pick up the phone. The same old songs rang through my mind. My insides shook. I could hear his voice. Sometimes I played the widow, no longer living, half-dead from the pain of being one when the heart was needing two. But wasn't my fate worse? I had to live knowing he was alive somewhere, breathing and working and sleeping so comfortably in his bed. Without me.

I had waited long enough. I had been handed my prison sentence so long ago, by that Colonel What's His Face. A name lost to my memory now. He had been my judge and jury. I was guilty and had been given life, but I had done 'good' time.

As I sat in silence, I couldn't remember now

why it had been so important to wait. Even to the point where time had started to fade and the years morphed into minutes.

If I could just talk to him…if I could just talk to him.

Once more I put my hand on the receiver. It made me dizzy.

Thoughts went back to how Harris saw fate. I recall the words he said, "Love comes first and providence takes care of the rest." Providence, my old enemy. I can't let go of that which I fear. And still I know, no one waits forever, except me. No one remains alone, but me. No one waits. Faced with the ultimate act of faith, finger on the trigger, I back away before I dial the number. I mouth the words, "Not yet. Not yet."

Chapter 40

Sometimes, you just do things and you don't know how or why this is the moment you've decided to do it. That is how my call to Harris happened.

I had been avoiding it for months before I actually put finger to phone, and at the same time I had been trying to get it accomplished for just as long. Nothing was cooperating with me. Not time, nor pride, not success, nor career. Facing his rejection stopped me even when I felt I couldn't go on another day without hearing his voice.

For a while, I thought of just calling the number and hanging up, just to see if he still lived there. Or if a woman answered. But I never managed to go through with it and so when the day finally arrived it shocked me more than it did him, I think.

It came quietly, sneaking up without warning or fanfare. A national holiday should have been declared, or at least I should have seen a full moon that night, but there was nothing to forewarn me. I leaned crosswise on the bed and plumped the mountain of pillows I had accumulated, one by one, under my face. My new room was magenta. Even when the guy at the paint store asked, "Are you sure you want to paint the whole room this color?" I never wavered. The pillows, almost the same color but in an Indian pattern of paisley, made me feel like I was sleeping in Jaipur.

I tufted and mussed until they gave way and molded to my liking. I took no time to think. I knew that would be the death of it. My phone sat on the nightstand, so quite calmly I laid down the magazine I was reading, reached over, picked up the receiver, and started pushing the buttons. I heard it ringing on the other end and then a voice, like a somewhat friendly ghost of summers past, spoke.

"Hello?"

"Harris?" I almost didn't recognize him. He was not as I had remembered. As much as l had loved, did love him, I could have called any number. I could have completely mistaken him for any man.

"Hi. This is Leah."

I had come too far to turn around now.

"How are you, Harris?"

"Okay," he said, but it was flat and

emotionless. Dry. I had hoped for more.

"I have some news." I started off with the story of Rose and Lance and their marriage. He said he had already heard. And then I told him about her kidney failure and that she had died.

"I'm sorry to hear that. I know you two were very close, but you know I left all of that behind when I left Clark. I really don't like to be reminded of it anymore. I'm just not the same person as I was then. I honestly don't know what it is you expect…."

"Oh, I don't expect anything." I lied. "I just wanted to reconnect with you and tell you that I have missed you."

"I'm touched by your feelings," he said sounding cold and hard. It wasn't the way I had known him. "I heard from my brother awhile ago that you contacted him. But when you didn't leave a number, well, I thought it was best to let the past remain in the past. I've moved on, Leah.'"

I didn't know how to explain to him why I hadn't called sooner. Telling him everything I had done in the past few years wasn't going to mean a thing to him. Trying to make him understand a decision I made in 1982 didn't make sense, either. He didn't sound receptive, not even to a casual conversation. If I had been able to articulate in that moment what I had wanted to say for so long, I would have simply told him I still loved him and regardless of what I had done and said, I never stopped.

The words came so much harder than I thought they would. I had played a version of our first conversation in my head over and over again, night after night for years, and it never went like this.

I asked him if he had met anyone.

"I have tried to have relationships since I knew you. It doesn't work out for me. I have given up on that part of my life as well. I don't want to do it, again. Not with you or anyone else. It's left a sour taste in my mouth. The word, *love,* is so misused. I'm not sure what it means anymore."

He didn't elaborate. The whole conversation lasted a quick eight minutes. It was only that long because I kept asking him questions. Hoping he would answer with more than a "Yes," "No," or "Okay." I was ready to hang up and call the whole thing a wash, when he reluctantly (at least that's how it felt) agreed to consider re-establishing some kind of friendship, although long distance. But he was adamant he wasn't looking for more.

It was all I got and I took it willingly.

Several more phone calls from both directions had taken place before it felt as if we were sliding back into a comfortable familiarity. He was almost always guarded. Afraid to say too much, but still willing to talk. Except there were the moments when I think he forgot and gave himself away. I lived for those slips. He unraveled his last several years by telling me the highs. Or in his case, it was more lows. He had moved to Seattle just after the Air Force. He named some jobs he had, but I quickly lost count. A library technician, a grocery store clerk, one job with the DMV, a bank customer service agent, a waiter at an upscale restaurant (which brought good tips) then a cook, two times as an aide for a political campaign, a video store assistant manager and a movie ticket seller. It was all so disappointing. I heard the sadness of failure in his story. He had moved as many times as he had jobs. To Montana and Wyoming, San Francisco and to Mexico where he lived in a spiritual commune for a year.

"I guess I've been lost. I still haven't found myself," he admitted to me one evening. I wanted to tell him that I could help. But I knew the time wasn't right. Not yet. He'd turn on me. He would run.

It felt as if I was coaxing a stray puppy, one who had been kicked by bullies in the street. I was only trying to feed and pet him, and give him a home, but he was wary. I had to be ever so gentle.

I gave a *Reader's Digest* version of my life

without him. I told him about the divorce. I was happy to make that announcement. I thought if anything were to change the future for us that would be it. But he hardly reacted to my news.

"That's good," he said. "I'm glad you finally did it. I know you'll be happier."

"Yeah, me too. I feel so much better now that it is over. Relieved. You know?"

No answer. Nothing for me to hang hope on.

"Harris, has your life turned out the way you expected?"

"I have no expectations, Leah. Those things are not a part of my consciousness now."

Again, so alienated, so estranged. I was facing the reality that we may never get beyond the hurt. The years without contact had pushed me and pulled me to believe that from the moment we spoke again we would declare undying love for each other and ride off together. I thought I would have my happy ending. I pictured it as clearly as if I had seen it at the movie theater. The trailer even came supplied with bumper music. Peabo Bryson's, *If Ever I'm in Your Arms Again.*

He had no expectations and I had expectations galore. But all of mine had to remain hidden for the time being. He didn't trust me yet. A day at a time. Infinitely small baby steps. I would have to prove that I would never hurt him again. He needed me to convince him.

At least the door had been opened. We were speaking again. If love was true it would still be there. It was still there, wasn't it?

The smell of mimosa and Harris's room flashed through my mind. I remembered the afternoon about three months after we met, when we sat in the middle of a field of grass on an old park bench. We had been out all day and the heat was blistering. My hair was wet and beads of sweat sat atop my nose. I wanted to cool off. I don't know why I remember this, but we both were wearing blue jean shorts. We never wore shorts. He led me to the bench and told me to lie down so that I could rest. I watched him walk away from me, to where a grove of coconut trees bent over and spread their leaves. Dry ones covered the ground underneath. I recall how exquisite he was to watch. Good breeding and bone structure. When I accused him of being handsome, he laughed at me, saying it was because he was Mestizo that I was fascinated by his looks. The mixture of Dutch, Indian, and Spanish gave him features more beautiful that a man was supposed to have.

He picked a large palm frond from the bunch and carried it to the bench. The next hour he fanned me, while he told me of his plans for the future. He said he would be a writer, possibly a poet, probably a novelist. He wanted to publish a book or two of poems by 30. He would finish college, studying English, and creative writing. Then he would write the novel. He could teach, too. And of course, we would have a house on a hill overlooking a lake. But those were the dreams of yesteryear. Not one of those things had he done. Now, he says he expects nothing from life.

I kept at it diligently. Trying to reel him in. But he never talked about feelings anymore. He instead talked about lack of feeling. Distance and purposelessness. He likened his life to being adrift at sea with no direction but knowing there was land somewhere. If he found it, great, and if he didn't, okay. That would be his fate.

Talk like that disturbed me. So many nights I wanted to tell him the story of our last goodbye. He never brought it up. He never even acted like we had been everything to each other once. Such a long, long time ago.

One night, when we had been discussing philosophy, I was excited and I sensed some joy in him as well. My body remembered the lusciousness of those talks we'd had in the past. The words included spirituality, direction, interpretation of dreams, meaning. It was the first conversation of its type for me since I had been by his side. For us, it was a natural way to talk. A place that might allow us to continue where we left off.

So I jumped in and said, "This takes me back to those days we sat on the floor in your room and talked about things like this. Remember that? It was such an easy relationship. You know we never fought did we?"

He was abrupt about putting me in my place. "Leah, we weren't together long enough to fight. You don't know what would have happened if we had lived in the same house. You need to be more realistic about what you remember."

I understood perfectly how things had been. It was Harris who had lost touch with reality. He was shielding himself from it so he wouldn't have to deal with it. I, on the other hand, had lived with it every day of my life for the past seven years.

Looking around the living room, I saw the chairs he sat on. He was all around me. The book he read, the pictures we looked at together. The talks we had about our childhoods. He was everywhere. I couldn't get away from him. Yet I had the feeling he had erased me from his life just as easily as he had wiped out the entire episode at Clark. He didn't want to revisit or reinvest in something so tucked away. I hung up the phone and pounded my fist against the end table. I cut my ring finger on the edge of the dresser. It stung like hell all night. I promised myself I would leave him be. He didn't want to hear about us. I wouldn't talk about us. In fact, I wouldn't call him again.

Chapter 42

Three days later, he was back. Saying things like: "Wouldn't it be nice to got together again. Oh, but just as friends, of course. But wouldn't it be great? Yes we should do that. Let's do it, soon." He wanted to make plans.

He sounded happy.

"Come on up here to Seattle. Yes, that is a wonderful idea. It's rainy and gray. You will love it. The chill is good for the soul."

"Yes. I will come. Of course, I will."

"When can you make it?" he asked.

"By the end of the month." I said, eager to jump before the spell wore off.

"That will be wonderful. Oh, but remember, no expectations of romance. You are a dear friend."

A dear friend? I was more than that and he knew it. I was the love of his life. I may have disappointed him and hurt him. His voice and every word that he had spoken told me that.

But he was softening. He started with a long distance friendship and from that moved to a meeting by the end of the month.

I was dreaming of the moment when our eyes would meet for the first time after years of separation. Dreaming seemed to be my specialty. I was in a perpetual state of living an alternate life. Harris was finally coming back to me. Or I was going to him. The feelings I had carried so deeply, for the one love in my past, would be reignited in us both. He could finally drop this shell of self-protection when he understood I would never betray him or love another.

I started making arrangements. I was going to Seattle to meet Harris. I started to believe. See, life can be fair, Mr. Brown. Good things do happen to good people.

I took out my 'plan book' and started sketching what I wanted to look like as I descended from the plane. I would need a new haircut, one that flattered my face and made me look as young as I was when I last saw him. I would first have to lose a few pounds. Not a ton, just a few pesky ones that hadn't been so important until the prospect of a weekend with Harris made them distasteful.

I needed to be more beautiful, more stylish, more alluring. Whatever he remembered about me could not compare to the new and improved model that had emerged. I had become somewhat successful as a career woman. A person with a vision. Then I shirked at the notion. Maybe I had done too much. All these years I had believed that while I was straightening out my life, he would be writing the novel, publishing his poems, or working as a professor somewhere. He had been close to finishing college when I left him. My plan was to accomplish as much as he had and then get back in touch. How would he feel now that I had found satisfaction in my career and was thriving? I had one almost-famous daughter, and another who was a student leader on campus.

Harris had nothing from what I could tell. He wasn't even working. I knew what to do. He could move down to LA and live with me. Sure, we had to be 'just friends,' but maybe I could help him. Encourage him to write. Maybe a screenplay. There were people who knew people…folks in literary. I would help get it sold. He wouldn't have to go adrift any longer.

Yes, that was a good plan. I needed to be humble, but helpful. At my best in every way so that he would have no choice but to fall in love all over again, at first sight.

When I told Jessie of my plans to meet Harris, her young romantic side came to light.

"Oh Mom, I can't wait. It's going to be so

great. It's like a fairy tale. You and Harris. Only now you really can get married and live happily ever after. He could move here, huh?"

I didn't tell her I had it all arranged in my head.

"I haven't gotten that far," I lied through my teeth.

Actually, I had even planned a wedding. The one I wanted when I married the wrong Mike. I didn't have my wedding because I was ashamed of marrying him, and didn't want anyone to be there. It wasn't a celebration. It was an arrangement.

But this would be different. We would marry outdoors. In the fall. It had to be fall. Maybe at Big Bear. Or Lake Arrowhead, where the air was cool and crisp, and I would wear burgundy regardless of what the rulebook says, or even a maroon print. My black curls would hang around my shoulders in the back and just a few tendrils would touch my cheeks in front. But there would be nothing foofy because I hated that 'put together' look. It had to be more casual than the typical nuptials.

We would share our own written vows. His would be poetry and mine would be dramatic, but so sincere. I hadn't figured out the music, but Journey's "Open Arms" came to mind. So did "Tahitian Moon" by Michael Franks. Pine fragrance and rosemary. Mint tea and

Moroccan tents. I wouldn't plan it all. Harris had definite ideas. I would leave parts for him. We would honeymoon somewhere in the Pacific. But not Hawaii, it was too cliché. Maybe Micronesia or Malaysia. Then, I would rescue him from his sadness and distrust, and no sooner would we settle down, he'd start writing, again. I would keep working in Hollywood, and we would buy a nice condo in the hills. Later, our place in the mountains. For the holidays. Dana's career and my clients still had to be looked after, so I needed to be in Los Angeles, but I knew I could make a way for Harris to be part of the whole new world I had created for myself.

"It's great Mom. You deserve it. Anything is possible, now," Jessica told me. "It could really happen."

I starved myself on this concoction of lemon juice, cayenne pepper, and maple syrup. A *fast,* they call it. I called it torture. It was fast all right. I dropped 14 pounds with speed, dizziness, and endless trips to the bathroom. And with that *fait accompli,* I promptly dispatched myself to the swankiest stylist in Beverly Hills just to get the perfect haircut. Money had not turned me into the upscale hair salon type, and I felt my throat close when I paid the bill, especially knowing that two years before, I would have had to spend that money on gas, food and rent.

Dana and Jessie wanted to go with me to the Sherman Oaks Fashion Square. They said I needed help picking my go–to-meet outfit. They were unabashedly on a makeover mission to give me more 'style.' In my mind, a trip to the mall was bad enough, but Dana wanted to go too, and as much as I hated to say it, the thought of her in a mall was just plain painful.

It had to be a covert operation if we were to get in and out without being noticed. The best way to avoid crowds was to sneak in early in the morning on a Sunday and get it over with by noon. It turned out to be a pretty good plan too, as we were only stopped once, by a mom who wanted Dana's autograph for her little girl. Of course, there were still the stares, and the folks who pretended not to see. But I always caught them peeking at us through their peripheral vision. It is the price you pay if you want to have your face plastered on TV. Dana didn't mind it much anymore. It was Jessie and I who were peeved. We weren't 'sort of famous' at all, and yet we still got the fallout from her celebrity.

Jessie found the cutest red dress, which I didn't want to try on, but did anyway just to make her happy. It did wonders for the olive in my complexion. I never really was a dress type. I kept telling the girls I thought a pair of jeans and a trendy shirt would be better.

"Oh, my God, Mom. You can't be serious. You are not going to see Harris after all this time wearing a pair of jeans."

I personally didn't see anything wrong with that idea. But I was vetoed and the dress was in. Shoes came next and they both decided I had to wear heels. That is when I used my own veto power. No way was I going to put on a pair of shoes I couldn't walk in. My girls had not seen me in stockings and heels and they weren't going to if I could help it. Never mind the grand reunion. I wasn't becoming a whole new person. I just wanted to be a bit more fixed up version of the person I knew.

I compromised and bought some great boots. Dana called them combat boots, but I had combat boots and these were nothing like them. With a dress, boots, earrings, and purse, I was more than done.

At the travel agent's office I plopped down another couple hundred dollars. It had turned into an expensive trip. I should have felt guiltier about spending so much, but I was beyond that. Mania had taken hold and I was becoming invincible. Everything would work out just perfectly, without a doubt. It had to. Once the ticket was paid for and the clothes picked out, hair and nails done to perfection, I called Harris to give him details of the trip.

"I'll be there on the 27th at 6:54 PM. Coming in on Southwest."

"Yeah…uh…."

"Is that alright?" Even though he had invited me, I wondered if I was being too pushy.

"No…I… It's just that… Leah, look… I have been thinking about this and I think you know I was deeply hurt by the things that happened between us. I felt betrayed by you and I just don't think I can ever trust you again. You lied to me. Our whole relationship was a lie."

"Harris, listen…."

"This is hard enough, Leah. Let me finish."

"I thought I could put it aside and go on, rekindle at least a friendship with you. I valued our friendship so much I wanted that back again. But I can't do it. I'm sorry. I don't want to get angry with you so I think this should be the last communication that we have. Let the past just stay in the past. I can't go through it again."

Then without so much as a goodbye he hung up the phone.

Chapter 43

The years came and went, doing me an unexpected favor. Tears that pooled got stuck before falling. Nothing about the call to Harris or its conclusion shocked me. It was nothing was I unprepared for. So many nights of pouring my heart into my pillow left me a bit like him. I have crusted over in places and the wounds, though not completely healed, are not as fresh as they had been. They don't ooze and burn like they had so long ago.

I stared out the window of my third story bedroom watching the people move along on the street below. Tops of heads with shoes and shirts. Couples who walked hand in hand. Others who walked alone. I could have been one of the faceless forms. I was, in someone else's point of view. Hiding a lifetime of secrets under my hat and shoes.

Who down there knew my type of pain? Who knew the joy of love so grand that it colored the world in a soft haze? So mighty it stopped your breath and begged you to die in its grasp? Who knew that feeling? Or dared to love with the intensity I did?

I grieved because I never told Harris why we turned out this way.

Why we only had the Philippines. Make no mistake, a smidgen of hope still held fast. In a tucked away dream that came to me in the off hours, or on the night when I had finally exorcised him from my conscious thoughts, I would see him on a farm somewhere in hilly terrain. Living in a cabin. Surrounded by fir and eucalyptus. And I would watch, stalking, as he made his way through a day, unaware I was following him. Or on other nights he would appear next to me in bed holding me tightly, kissing my neck, and rocking with my body until I was reborn. Mornings after those dreams, I was fuzzy with hope and possibilities floated through me making me believe in that 'one day.'

But mostly, I needed to set things straight. I had a responsibility to tell him. How though, could I approach a man who said to me, "Let this be our last communication." Was the telling more for him, or for me? Was I granted absolution, three Hail Marys and an Our Father if I confessed? What right did I have to bother him when he had laid down the rules.

HE DIDN'T WANT TO HEAR FROM ME.

At 7:00 PM one summer evening, I made a decision.

Then I began I counting down the hours. At 8:39 PM, I looked at the clock. It had been one hour and 39 minutes since I decided the words Michael (Harris) Harrison would be permanently and irrevocably erased from my mental dictionary.

I went to the kitchen and fumbled through every cupboard looking for some forbidden snack to fill the empty space that grew exponentially larger by the minute. After two hours and 18 minutes, I called Pizza Man and ordered a large vegetarian pizza–no garlic, no onions.

Three hours and five minutes after my decision, the deliveryman rang the buzzer. I paid for the food, happy that Dana was out so I didn't have to share, and I started gobbling the slices so fast I hardly chewed.

I became fascinated with the Elvis clock, the one where his legs dangle as it ticks. Perched above an antique steamer trunk that took up the space in front of my bed, I watched it, becoming dizzy. Tick tock, jailhouse rock.

Exactly four hours since I declared I would never talk to or about the person whom shall henceforth remain nameless, and I was bloated, pacing the floor between the bedroom and the hall closet and, perhaps the only coherent sentences going through my head were idiotic ideas. I envied drug addicts in that moment. They didn't have to deal with life sober. At least they could have snorted or shot up, popped a few pills or smoked some weed. I had come to the point where a bit of mind altering help would have been a welcome relief.

Four hours and 22 minutes. Dana called to ask if she could spend the night at the photography director's house. She and his daughter, Monica, had become fast friends. So it was either Dana there or Monica here. I was happy to oblige.

At four hours and 50 minutes, Elvis had driven me to the point of lunacy. I dug through the pile of clothes in my laundry bag and pulled out a Levi Jacket that hadn't seen the light of day for months. Purse over my shoulder and a ball cap on my head, I was out the door, walking as fast and furiously as I could. Past Olsen's Coffee Shop, past the trendy boutique, past the vintage clothing store, the art gallery, the herbal supply, the Ralph's grocery store. In fact, I didn't come to a full stop until I was in the middle of the North Hollywood Liquor Store on the corner and in the aisle where Gin, Vodka, Rum, and Whiskey were lined up in color collation. Not remembering what a Margarita was made of, I inspected the bottles to see if there were recipes on the labels. It had to be Margaritas. A tribute to Rose, to the nameless one, and to my patience, effort, never-ending devotion and undying love. As embarrassing as it was, I ended up asking the guy behind the counter, who I could tell by the turban was Sikh, how to make one. He gave me a look that made me wish I had gone looking for the local pusher instead, but he pointed me in the direction of the 'ready-made' versions. That was all I needed. Two bottles in a bag later I was walking back from whence I came with just as much speed and purpose.

If he didn't want to hear my voice, fine. He had a right not to answer me if I called. I knew he had caller ID so he might not. But a letter, a good old-fashioned letter to explain the night we ended. The parts with him (WH), and the parts after him (AH). There were no parts that didn't include him. So I twisted open the first bottle of Toma del Santos Margarita, and poured a water glass full. My mind lingered too long over my lack of an appropriate vessel to use for a tribute.

But it was the thought that counted and even a Dixie cup would have done the trick. In fact, it might have been more poignant.

"I must get ready," I said to myself. "I need a pen and stationery."

I caught myself laughing out loud. I hadn't

had anything but business stationary since I started working at the agency.

I took the computer printer paper from my desk. I considered writing the whole letter on the computer because I type faster than I write. I always seem to have my thoughts running ahead of my hand if I use a pen. But this letter needed to be handwritten. When he opened it he would see that the words were crafted by the hand he kissed. The one he held. The one that held him.

I sipped at the Margarita. It was bitter and lemony. It reminded me of the *cerveza con limón* that I drank the night that we fell into each other. The night I fell from grace. Rose. The Officer's Club after school. The balmy breezes of Angeles City. Another city of angels. On the patio where live musicians and local singers belted out love songs. Rose and I at a rattan table with white cloth napkins and citronella candles in the center. The air was so thick you could grab it in your fingers and hold the warmth. The typhoons were coming, Rose said. And it's true, they were.

How do I start?

I must use his name, again.

One more time.

Dear Harris,

I love you. From the moment I saw your blue shirt with the rolled up sleeves, I suspected it. Though you hadn't seen me, I felt ions inside changing. When our eyes first met, I no longer wondered, I dare to say, nor did you. In that instant our spirits mingled and found the half that had been searching for its twin. No greater feeling have I known in this life than the merging of our souls as my heart became yours. Each day now is colored by your memory. Each moment is lived with the hope that there is a heaven, or at least another life beyond this temporary one on Earth. I pray that it is so for one reason only. That God will place us side by side again.

Before you there was pain and torment and unhappiness. All I longed for was love and fulfillment. Pieces of me were floating out in the universe waiting for the glue to make them whole. I had beautiful children whom I worshiped. But the truth is until you came, my heart didn't know a thing about love. It imitated and acted. But it never understood.

But, one day, that beautiful perfect rainy day, when you were trying with what little you had, to create a haven for me and the kids, I was summoned to the office of the base commanding officer. He told me I had to make a choice. No, choice is the wrong word, it was an ultimatum. He talked to me of Article 15s and court marshals. He warned me of the consequences for both of us. I was to be sent home. Alone. Without Jessie and Dana. An unfit mother he said. They would stay with their father.

He stared me square in the eye when he assured me if I did not leave you, you would be dealt with in the most serious manner that the Uniformed Code of Military Justice allowed.

But, finally, he handed me the olive branch. He said if I would cut all contact, never see you again, and return to my husband, as his wife, with complete dedication to my marriage, I would be allowed to stay. I would be allowed to stay with my girls.

With the same sternness he also said you wouldn't be called before him or anyone else, as long as I did 'the right thing.'

That was the night you came to the back door in the pouring rain. The night you beamed with pride over finding the perfect home for us. When both of us were taken to a place darker and more vile than any hell I can imagine.

I was scared. Afraid if I told you what had happened, you would have done something terrible. Maybe more terrible even than the tormented years you have been through not knowing.

Yes, it's true, like a Judas, I betrayed you. I was going back to my husband. You said that was crazy, you knew I didn't love him. You were right. I loved you. More than I even realized then. I loved you. But the words that came from me, tore us apart at the core of our being. You would only go away if I told you the big lie. As much as I wanted to say I would never leave you, and I would endure anything to keep us as one, I did the unthinkable.

The words have stabbed at me over and over again. They cut deeper as the years went by. So many years. So many cuts. There is no love left in me at all, if it is not for loving you. If you had only known what I really felt.

Silently, each night I begged for your forgiveness.

Now you say our love was based on betrayal and lies. Yes, I did lie. And yes I did betray. But only on the surface. Not in my heart. Not where it counted.

Your cries as you rode away that night still haunt me. In the strangest times I hear them. When I am driving to work, the sound of the cars turn into you screaming "NO." I hear them when I am listening to a sweet slow song. And sometimes when I see a bicycle, or a man in a uniform.

What became of you after that night, is what became of me. In you it may look different, but we were equally fractured. No man can put back what has been put asunder. We are still intertwined in each other's souls. You said we came to Earth as twin flames. Two bodies one soul. We found each other in this big wide world. That in itself is the miracle. In this lifetime we touched passion and had a love that so many sing about, and write about and talk about, and so few have known.

So you may have decided that you never want to talk to me again, I understand. You have been damaged. I am responsible for that. Damage caused by inconceivable beauty. We stand apart and perhaps must walk the rest of this life's path alone. I don't know why it had to be this way, except I remember once when we were lovers, you said that passions so vast, so fierce, so consuming cannot sustain themselves and thus the great lovers of the world all die in agony.

Is this our fate? Are we to play out a Shakespeare tragedy? If so, I am resigned now to that ending. We move through our lives, now alone, but as we do, keep this thought under your breast, deep in your heart, beyond human sentiment. You are loved. You will always be loved.

Please forgive me.
Leah

Epilogue

Last night, I drank my coffee on the patio before the sun rose. Another night watching stars play against the blackened sky and I know it is only insomnia that causes me to count the hours before dawn. But I cherish these hours. They are solemn and still. My voice is louder when the rest of the world is quiet. I came outside to sit on the old metal chair. It isn't the most comfortable chair on my balcony, but it is a seat for my thoughts. It has taken on the imprint of moments spent looking forward and back, and it carries that energy. The wrought iron is familiar to the touch. We have spent many nights together in communion.

My cup says Starbucks Lebanon. A souvenir of travel to another place along the journey. I look at the old table as I rest my arms against its bumpy texture.

Rescued from a junk shop in Orange County, I made a random mosaic on top of cracked plates and glass. Another project to occupy my mind. Staring at the patterns and pieces, I am thinking I should have decoupaged or collaged the table instead. Used the bits of my past that are stuck in boxes, in the back of my chest of drawers. Things I have to unpack to recall how they entered my life. I like to live with things that make me remember. No need to have items bought which carry no significance. My puka shell lamp, my silly Starbucks cup, the pillow covers from my summer in Thailand. Jessica's veterinary school graduation photograph. The canopy that hangs over my bed bought on that six-hour trip to Morocco. Dana's Young Actor of the Year Award.

My degree from the Film Institute of America.

These are the things my life has made. I should have pasted ticket stubs and programs, pictures and movie reviews. My father's obituary, Jessica's wedding invitation. Those are not random. Everything has purpose at this time in the morning. Every beat of a heart has its reason for still carrying on. We may not know who will cross our path and change us, or how our lives will evolve, but we all know we are on a mission. Even as an astronaut or a mountain climber moves higher and farther, so do we.

In the middle of the night, it is easy to believe that the purpose for my being is glorious and I am here to change the world and usher in a new and better Earth. A Buddha complex, a Jesus wish. But I really see that I am just a little cog in the wheel and maybe my purpose is just be the best cog, doing the best job that I have been appointed to do.

Back In 1982, shortly after arriving in the Philippines, Rose and I took a drive down MacArthur highway to Dau. Way before McDonald's and Pizza Huts erupted and put all of the quaint little restaurants out of business. We lunched at the Caribou Café where a guy named Romy cooked the world's best spring rolls and fried rice. Filipino fried rice. Not your garden variety Chinese type. Eaten with Marco Pina soy sauce. The dark aroma of the sauce and frying vegetables filled the room. It was ecstasy in food form. We watched the girls in skintight jeans and heels, and the GI boys who married them and took them home to the USA, but never told anyone how they met their wives. We were transplants from Ohio and New York, thrown together by fate or folly because our husbands had sworn their allegiances to the US Air Force, and though we each admitted we thought about not going with them, we had somehow known to make the journey when they were ordered to serve at

Clark. That day in the Caribou, it was not as hot as most in Pampanga, but it was February and that year in February the heat took respite. We had a real winter. We wore jackets of wine and grey.

We poked at our egg rolls with chopsticks, looking like two normal married women, but both of us had recently crossed over into a new realm. We had left the mere mortals who surrounded us and we were giddy with the prospect of our new loves. Yes, we were well aware of our moral shortcomings. We knew what we were doing was off limits, wrong and adulterous. Yet neither of us felt it to be as wrong as the rulebook said it was. In the highest tradition of romance, we had been swept into a whirlpool that we were unable to calm. No premonition had prepared us for those first class sessions. In some strange uncanny twist of fate, on the same night, at the same moment we instantly recognized the two men who were certainly our soul mates.

Lance, with his tall dark good looks could have been a football player for the NFL. He was as broad across the shoulders as he was tall. To see him in a doorway could instill fear in a man of lesser stature. Lance was a knight of the most honorable order, like his namesake. A man of true heart and stalwart loyalty. His devotion to Rose unwavering. She sensed she had found the one person who would be able to handle what she already suspected her future held. To his credit, he never flinched or ran from the burden she placed upon him. He stood by her until the end.

Life is a series of comings and goings. Decisions, which seem small, make the biggest changes. Lance and Rose, Harris and I. Every step we each took drove us closer to acting out a plan more charged with destiny than anything we could have imagined for ourselves.

For so long, I have tried to let go, to go on. To be without him. To look for love, again. To be whole.

But wholeness requires that all parts be present, and for me that isn't possible since the most important part, the part that holds my heart has been torn away.

I'm not surprised we didn't reunite. I probably knew what I couldn't admit back then. I would know love only for a blink in the eye of time.

Harris told me he would rather be alone. Put the past where it belonged. So here we are, both alone. The two of us living and dying while needing the other. Instead of crossing the plank that would bridge the gap, we are separated by the years of hurt. My mistake, his mistake. Our fate.

Is love so close to hate that I am the enemy? Could he not see that I had no choice? There are days when I still cry. But mostly now I love my life. Because even though I am doomed to be without Harris, I do have a life. And it's a much better one than I could have imagined for myself, considering how it got sidetracked and off course in the beginning. I am grateful. But I am always aware of the loss, an empty side of the bed, the pain of a love that consumed us both then spit us out.

I drift away to the place I have longed for. I feel his breath on mine. I open my eyes to see if he is close. I feel a touch. It mixes with sleep and once again I am dreaming of him. We are walking together on Signal hill. The day is bright and only marshmallow clouds dot the perfect blue of the Philippine sky. He sits with me in the tall grass, under the mimosa tree, and I hold him gently, with care, to see if he will break. I tell him how I missed him, and that I never gave up hope. He assures me he loved me always.

No matter what he said, no matter the pain, we are now together for eternity. Off in the distance, I recognize two figures emerging from a field of honeysuckle and hydrangeas. Rose is walking with Lance by her side. She raises a hand to greet us. I wait for them to get closer, but they move towards us for what seems like hours. Covering no ground, they never reach our hill. I think I have died. I look for signs I am still alive. Still breathing.

I turn to Harris. I touch the side of his face and stroke his hair. I smell the cologne he wore all those years ago and my body aches with desire for him once more. I am whole again. As we kiss, I am awakened by the alarm.

Sun peeks over the houses in the distance. The rustling of cars starts, building in its cadence as the morning rush begins.

It has been a long, long time. My curls have given way to a short bob that replaces their bounce. The bounce in my walk has been replaced too, by time, and a surefootedness that has allowed me to be stable and secure and confident in my ability to make my own way.

I will have another morning. Rose will not. My father will not. Others I have known have also fallen away. But I am still here.

When daylight brightens my bedroom, I turn on the computer and check the blog of Colin Harrison. He talks about writing. His writing. Six novels, two that have been turned into major motion pictures. We ran across each other at a premier once. I knew him immediately. He had never met me. He didn't even realize it when I stood next to him. Of course I was looking for someone else, but that Harrison was nowhere in sight. Their mother was present, so as I watched mother and son, I found myself thinking there should be another son, and I should be standing next to that one. I should be a part of their family. It was obvious why he was absent. The irony wasn't lost on me. As much as I wanted to, I didn't dare ask what had happened to the brother. So each day, I read the blog. Praying that Harris will be mentioned in passing. He never is.

Before getting ready for work, I open the drawer. The one in my bed stand. The one with all the memories. Carefully. I inspect the envelope. Looking at the address, I wonder if he lives there anymore. I'm certain he doesn't. The corners of the flap are turned slightly. A stain has dried on the back. Probably coffee from one of the times I clutched it too long in my hand. His name still makes me tingle when I see it in print. I realize the stamps are no good any more. How many times has the cost of mail gone up since then?

It's time to go.

I carry the letter to the trashcan in the corner of my room and hold it over the opening, daring myself to let loose.

This should be over now.

If I could just drop it.

I am almost there.

Then an image in my bookcase makes me pause.

The blue linen cover of the only book I have kept through all of my moves. I reach for it. Fanning the pages, I smell the passage of time. The heat, typhoon season and mangoes flood my senses. I open to the center of the book where the binding is worn from the many times I've read about the young yogi who sought God and left his homeland to follow his destiny. I flatten the paper and lovingly place the letter in the care of the *Autobiography of a Yogi*.

Sitting in the Caribou Café outside Clark Air Base on that balmy afternoon in February of 1982, Rose took another bite of her spring roll, pointed her finger at me and said, "You know what I think, Loca?

"Tell me, what do you think, Rose?" I laughed for no reason at all.

A single tear escaped to fall against her cheek.

She leaned in.

"I think we are the luckiest two women in the entire world."

I still believe she was right.

About the Author

Thank you for letting me introduce you to the world of Leah Holden.

She is a good example of a woman who has had to learn about two words that play an important part in my life. On the inside of each of my wrists I have a tattoo. Small, written in white ink so no one but me can see them, I had PERSEVERE needled on my left, and FORGIVE placed on the right. They were supposed to be daily reminders of the two things I needed to do most in this world and the two things I found hardest to achieve.

In the beginning I thought about those tattoos daily, especially during the itchy healing period! But like all new fascinations, they became old and ordinary after a few months, and I simply stopped noticing them.

When I started writing my book *The Sympathy of All Things* a few years ago, like a lot of new authors I stopped and started, and stopped and started again.

Plenty of times I felt like I would never finish, because I didn't know if I had what it takes to see it to the finish line. But the truth is, the only reason my book exists today is because I did persevere. Not brilliantly, or with any type of superpower, but like most humans do. Taking itty, little baby steps, one at a time.

Because I am an artist, a teacher, a spiritual seeker, and an absolute believer in world travel, you will find my upcoming stories almost always have a kernel of me at the core. A little bit of spirituality, art, or travel will probably be buried deep in the pages. Since I have persevered and forgiven myself for taking so long to complete *The Sympathy of All Things*, I am now ready begin again.

My next book, to be released in 2014, is about my journey with Multiple Sclerosis. Definitely a different type of journey, than the type Leah took . I am often traveling through pain, and sometimes limitation and inconvenience. But having MS is also a big part of the reason why I have those tattoos on my wrist. With MS everyday means another day of persevering to just do what 'normal' folks do without thinking. I live with it, but I think having it has taught me how to live.

Like most people I take the good with the bad, but I am determined to learn how to exemplify the meaning of my tattoos. Like Leah says, "life offers us no guarantees." I am a firm believer in this. We may not be able to change some things about our fate or destiny, but we certainly can work with what we are given.

Acknowledgement

A huge thanks to the staff of New Way Press for their unending support and guidance as I took this book from paper to publication.

To my first readers Kaneez Iqbal and Judy Reesha for their comments and feedback that allowed me to understand the writing from the readers point of view.

A special thanks to Valerie Haynes-Perry for her editorial expertise. The time and attention she paid to the details and flow of the writing truly helped me to become a stronger story teller.

To all family and friends who believed in my ability to finish this work even though sometimes I doubted myself, I say:

I love you.

www.ingramcontent.com/pod-product-compliance
Lightning Source LLC
La Vergne TN
LVHW050929080826
845145LV00001B/274

* 9 7 8 0 6 1 5 8 7 5 9 6 5 *